A Prequel

BREACH!

CORINNA TURNER

unSeen

PRAISE FOR CORINNA TURNER'S BOOKS

LIBERATION: nominated for the *Carnegie Medal Award 2016.*
ELFLING: 1st prize, Teen Fiction, *CPA Book Awards 2019*
I AM MARGARET & *BANE'S EYES:* finalists, *CALA Award 2016/2018.*
LIBERATION & *THE SIEGE OF REGINALD HILL:* 3rd place, *CPA Book Awards 2016/2019.*

PRAISE FOR *ELFLING*

I was instantly drawn in

EOIN COLFER, author of *Artemis Fowl* and former Children's Laureate of Ireland.

PRAISE FOR *DRIVE!*

*What a terrifying futuristic world Turner has created!
I am a huge fan of this author and am always impressed
with how different all her stories are. Look forward to
the next one in this series!*

LESLEA WAHL, author of award-winning *The Perfect Blindside*

A cross between Jurassic World *and* Mad Max!
*Fun, fast paced. And sets up an incredible new world.
I read it three times in two days!*

STEVEN R. MCEVOY, BookReviewsAndMore Blogger
and Amazon Top 500 Reviewer

Wow! So suspenseful you won't be able to put it down!

KATY HUTH JONES, author of *Treachery and Truth*

Jurassic Park *fans will love this short!*

CAROLYN ASTFALK, author of *Rightfully Ours*

*Very short, but extremely exciting. ... The action is brutal, but it
drags you in and doesn't let you go until you hit the last page.*

ASHLEY STANGL

ALSO BY CORINNA TURNER:

I AM MARGARET series
For older teens and up

Brothers *(A Prequel Novella)**
1: I Am Margaret*
1: Io Sono Margaret (Italian)
2: The Three Most Wanted*
3: Liberation*
4: Bane's Eyes*
5: Margo's Diary*
6: The Siege of Reginald Hill*
7: A Saint in the Family
'The Underappreciated Virtues of Rusty Old Bicycles' *(Prequel short story) Also found in the anthology:*
Secrets: Visible & Invisible*

I Am Margaret: The Play *(Adapted by Fiorella de Maria)*

UNSPARKED series
For tweens and up

Main Series:
1: Please Don't Feed the Dinosaurs
2: A Truly Raptor-ous Welcome
3: PANIC!*
4: Farmgirls Die in Cages*
5: Wild Life
6: A Right Rex Rodeo
7: FEAR†

Prequels:
BREACH!*
A Mom With Blue Feathers†
A Very Jurassic Christmas*
'Liam and the Hunters of Lee'Vi'

FRIENDS IN HIGH PLACES series
For tweens and up

1: The Boy Who Knew (Carlo Acutis)*
2: Old Men Don't Walk to Egypt (Saint Joseph)*
3: Child, Unwanted (Margaret of Castello)

Do Carpenter's Dream of Wooden Sheep? *(Spin-off, comes between 1 & 2)*

1: El Chico Que Lo Sabia (Spanish)
1: Il Ragazzo Che Sapeva (Italian)

YESTERDAY & TOMORROW series
For adults and mature teens only
Someday: A Novella*
Eines Tages (German)
1: Tomorrow's Dead†

OTHER WORKS

For teens and up
Elfling*
'The Most Expensive Alley Cat in London' *(Elfling prequel short story)*

For tweens and up
Mandy Lamb & The Full Moon*
The Wolf, The Lamb, and The Air Balloon *(Mandy Lamb novella)*

For adults and new adults
Three Last Things *or* The Hounding of Carl Jarrold, Soulless Assassin*
A Changing of the Guard

The Raven & The Yew†

† **Coming Soon**
* **Awarded the Catholic Writers Guild** *Seal of Approval*

1

BREACH!

Time: 19 years before the main unSPARKed series.

Beep.

Beep.

Beep.

The persistent noise draws me sluggishly from sleep, dumping me not into full wakefulness but into a stomach-clenching memory of that morning—an alarm clock waking me, my head thumping, no idea where I was, panic quickly giving way to a bone-deep regret and a shame that still clings to me like dirt...

Argh, that was over two months ago, just after my eighteenth birthday. Late February now and I've put it behind me. Lesson learned and all that. Yeah, I'm good at learning from my mistakes. If I wasn't, I'd have been eaten by now.

And that beep isn't some city dweller's alarm clock;

it's the HabVi's console. In fact, it's—

I sit up so fast I bang my head on the roof of my little overCab bedroom—this is the spacious "Master" bedroom in newer Habitat Vehicles, but in our old banger it's almost as pokey as the shelf bunk in the living area, where I slept for five years.

Breach alarm. But not *our* breach alarm. Grabbing my rifle from alongside my sleeping bag, I check the dim screen beside the bunk door anyway, but the living area looks normal. Jumping out without even glancing at the footholds, I land easily on the metal floor and dart to the console, pulling a sweater on.

Yes, a nearby farm has a breach. In fact—*Oh no!*

I slap my hand on the "open" button of the cab without knocking. "Zech!" The door slides open and I dive into the driver's seat, dumping my rifle beside me and whacking the sleeping-bag-swaddled feet on the seat-bed beside it. "Zech, can't you hear the alarm? Get up!" I open the cab's solid metal shutters, raise the stabilizers, and deploy the mirrors with three quick button flicks, then turn the ignition key. "There's a breach nearby!"

"All right, all right, Isaiah." A huge yawn, and my older brother's tousled black hair appears at the top of his sleeping bag, along with a glimpse of brown skin and sleepy brown eyes very like my own.

"It's that *tourist resort*, Zech!"

"Argh, *outage*!" Zech jack-knifes into a sitting position, still swearing. Really swearing. I know how he feels, but...

"Zech!" I glance meaningfully at our little statue of Saint Desmond on the dashboard. "Now, seriously?" He'll really cheese Saint Des off just when we're heading into a breach situation?

Zech snorts. "Yeah? After New Year's Eve, you can't talk." But he mouths "sorry" at the statue before rolling off the bed and grabbing his pants.

I let off the parking brake, then spin the wheel and press the accelerator, sending the 'Vi roaring up a steep slope and Zech tumbling back into his bed, headfirst.

"Isaiah!"

"Why don't you just sleep with your pants on like any sane hunter?"

"I like a bit of ventilation, cub."

"Oh, just get them on before you scare all the city-ladies." Cub, indeed. At twenty-one, he's only three years older than me.

At the reminder of the potentially dire situation we face, Zech lies on his back with his legs in the air and manages to wriggle into the pants, despite the fact that I'm driving at break-neck speed up the slope and down into the next valley. Then he grabs the Intercar mic. "What's the place called?"

"Er, Green Meadows or something, I think."

"Hello, Green Meadows Resort or whatever you are, this is the Wilson HabVi, what is your situation?"

Nothing but static. The resort's always stuffed full of noisy cityfolk and we've never been inside. We shot a juvenile edmontosaur within sight of their fence once, and some manager fellow rushed out in a truck and begged us to take it away and *butcher it somewhere else*, shoving a wad of cash into Zech's hand before we could point out that obviously we were going to pull it *inside* the 'Vi first. Butchering carcasses near resorts could be a nice little earner, clearly, but it feels too like extortion—kinda would be, I guess—so we've kept our distance since then.

Once we're over the next rise, Zech tries again. "Hello, Green Meadows Resort or whatever the name, this is the Wilson HabVi, what is your situation?"

"HabVi? Did you say *HabVi?*" The hysterical voice blasts from our speakers, making Zech turn them down quickly. "Are you hunters?"

"Yeah, we're hunters. What's the problem?"

"T. rex. There's a *T. rex*. It came straight through the electric fence; now it's wandering around, it's *roaring!*"

Zech rolls his eyes at me. Yeah, the poor beast's probably feeling well singed. "Roaring, huh? Is it doing anything else?" One singed rex looks fearsome but is unlikely to cause much trouble unless someone decides to run under its nose. "Did you get everyone inside?"

"How? Raptors came through the breach almost at once. They're everywhere. I keep broadcasting for people to *stay inside*, but every time the rex goes near a chalet someone panics and tries to run. The raptors—they're *eating* them."

No smile on Zech's face now. A resort full of helpless cityfolk, children too, no doubt...and raptors. "*Make* people stay inside," he snarls. "The rex is unlikely to try and get into a building, unless there's somewhere with a whole lotta food. And if your chalets are built to regulation, it'll take the raptors ages to breach one. So *make them stay inside!*"

"They're not listening to me..."

"Who are you, anyway? Can I speak to the senior fence guard?"

"I *am* the fence guard. I'd just come out to do the morning check when the rex..."

Zech huffs. The guy on the end of the Intercar doesn't seem very effective, for a fence guard. "Has anyone taken shelter in the dining room, kitchen, or food storage areas?"

"I don't know. I'm in the fence control booth."

"Get over there and check, then just drive back and forth and calm everyone down until we get there."

"I can't go *out*. There're raptors everywhere! I can't get to my vehicle."

Zech clenches his teeth. Yeah, he should've parked

his vehicle closer, shouldn't he? Incompetent, for sure. "Fine, put some steel into your voice and do it all via intercom. *Explain* it to them. Don't run from the rex. The rex is not the danger. The danger is the raptors. So they must stay inside. Help is on the way. Make them stay put."

"I'll try. But they're not listening—"

"We'll be there soon."

Zech cuts the connection and dumps the mic back into its cradle. "Fence guard? I wouldn't want him guarding a *nursery*."

"I guess the rejects from the SPARK Brigade have to work somewhere." Only the best are accepted by the elite force that guards and maintains the huge city fences; small private settlements like the resort hire their own.

"Just put your foot down, Isaiah."

"What does it look like I'm doing, Zechariah?"

I let the huge vehicle drift across a wide curve of gravel, accelerating again as we begin to straighten out. In fact, I keep the accelerator hard down, despite the fact that we're tearing up the sod and leaving an ugly brown trail.

Zech slips into a t-shirt and sweater and has just thrown his ammo sash on when we top another rise.

"There it is, Zech."

Zech grabs the binos from a torn door pouch and

focuses on the extensive settlement ahead. Extensive compared to the usual isolated farm, anyway. Rows of little chalets spread over the side of another gentle hill, with some bigger buildings at the summit. Manicured grounds down the back, I recall, and some more chalets.

A large shape moves, just visible over some of the chalets near the top, a testy roar carrying to our external mics.

"There's the rex." Zech's finger moves on the wheel of the binos. "Looks okay from here. Probably more shaken than anything. It's a juvenile male."

"What else would it be?"

"A juvenile female?"

"Not as often." But it's always a juvenile, that's for sure. Older rex know to stay away from electricity. If we can get this one out of there without killing it, it will know too. Which means getting it out alive is the highly preferred option. Otherwise the Dinosaur Activity and Population department (or DAPdep, as most people call it) will have to let another one hatch out—something's got to maintain a stable herbi'saur population, after all—and this will probably happen all over again, somewhere else, sooner than it need.

"What's the plan, Zech? Can you see the breach? Is it this side?"

Just the two of us to deal with a rex, at least one pack of raptors, and...how big a hole in the fence?

Zech scans the fence as we roar downhill like an armored juggernaut with massive wheels and huge tires. A rusty armored juggernaut.

"Ah, got it. Eight o'clock position. Looks like…hmm, from here I'd say a total breach, but no dragging to speak of."

Total breach, so the fence strands are actually broken right in two, but they haven't been dragged far out of position, so it's a fairly small, clean hole. It could be worse. Could be better, too, since a partial breach—with electrified wires still lying across the hole—would help keep the raptors out.

"Raptor count?"

"I've spotted Dakotaraptors and Utahraptors already, so at least two packs. And I think I mighta seen a velociraptor tail, but I couldn't swear to that one."

"*Three packs?*" I can't help shooting Saint Des a reproachful look. Is this my comeuppance for New Year? "This is going to be a fun day."

Zech grunts agreement. "First off, we're going to quickly drive up and down between all those chalets, looking big and mean and broadcasting that the hunters are here now so everything's fine; they just need to stay indoors until we've dealt with the situation."

I can't help snorting slightly at that, but still. The most urgent thing is to calm people down enough that they stop feeding themselves to the raptors.

"Then we'll figure out how to get the rex out. Then fix the fence. Then it's just a raptor hunt."

"Oh joy." *Yeah, we're going to need your help today, Saint Des.* Saint Desmond the Hermit—who lived alone in a cave for twenty years without being eaten by any of the local raptor packs—has been the staunch patron saint of hunters and all those who live unSPARKed—outside an electric fence—ever since he was canonized, shortly after Zech and I were born. If he's got our back, we'll be fine.

"Gate, Zech?" Fighting to keep the heavy vehicle on course, I don't want to mess with the Intercar myself.

"Resort, this is the HabVi, please open your gate."

"Oh, thank God! You're here!"

The outer gate slides open ahead of us. Once we're inside the gate compound, I slow to a crawl until the outer gate has swooshed shut and the inner one opened. Through we go.

I drive straight for the chalets but stare at the fence control booth near the gate as we pass—and at the vehicle parked right outside. What's the guy playing at, staying in there?

"What's your intercom frequency?" Zech asks the guard, his voice tight.

"Er...dunno."

Zech growls, his hand tightening around the mic. "Fine, patch me through!" He gives the guard a moment to fumble with his equipment as I head for the road between the first two rows of chalets, then demands, "Ready?"

"Uh, yeah."

Zech breathes out deeply, letting his frustration with the guard go, and speaks calmly and authoritative-ly. "Resort guests, this is the Wilson HabVi, we are taking charge of this situation. Please stay indoors until further notice. If the rex approaches your location, remain inside and it will walk on by. Raptors are loose in the resort, so under no circumstances go outside until further notice. Keep all doors and windows closed at all times. Resort guests, this is the Wilson HabVi..."

As I drive up and down the rows Zech keeps up his patter, sounding tough and chilled out, if not outright bored, just the way old Mister Wilson used to do it when we were younger. "Nothing calms panicked cityfolk like someone who's bored by a T. rex," he used to say. People wave from windows, faces naked with relief but no surprise, so the chalet's intercom system must be transmitting the message.

As we move higher up the hill, I slow down, not wanting to come up on the rex by accident. Zech, leaving a recording on loop setting, goes up to our observation turret for a better view. His rifle barks now and then as he picks off the odd raptor that doesn't zip out of sight fast enough. There's a risk the noise of gun and engines will attract the rex's attention, but they tend to hunt more by sight—movement, specifically. Thanks to something or other back when the foolish scientists first bred them—arrogantly assuming they, like the rest of their "restorations," would never escape—rex don't identify static objects as prey.

Crack, goes Zech's rifle again.

"Yeah, there's velociraptors, for sure." We've both slipped our earpieces in so we can talk to one another easily. "One less, now."

I sigh. "Great."

I glance at the dashboard screen, which displays the feed from the forward pointing turret-top camera. The rex isn't that far ahead, now, still stamping and roaring angrily, so far paying us no heed, but if we get too close it might get interested since we're a moving object and we're taller than the chalets. At about fourteen feet tall, the juvenile can see over them too. "Zech, I'd better cut around it now so we can do the other side of the hill."

"Yep."

I turn right, trying to picture the gentle curves of the lines of chalets and plot a course that will take us clear of Rexie. Everywhere we drive up here, frightened faces peer from chalet windows and feathery raptor tails whisk away around corners. Who in their right mind would run outside just now? But they do. Too scared of the rex to realize the greater danger.

"Isaiah, stop." Zech's voice comes sharply and the automated message playing into the Intercar mic cuts off as he silences it from the turret console above.

I ease us to a halt at once, glancing at the screen again as I cut the engine. The rex isn't in view on that cam but—a roar nearby—yes, it's moving closer to us. Coming to check us out? We'll have to wait for it to wander off again.

"Oh *outage, outage...*" Zech's soft, horrified whisper stands all the hair on the back of my neck on end.

There... A little girl stumbles from between two chalets, her face screwed up in absolute, silent terror. Those thudding footsteps speed up abruptly, a smashing sound in the distance as the rex pushes past something. It glimpsed her, and it's coming. I've jerked the door open and swung down into the fresh morning air before I can even think. "Zech, cover me."

"Isaiah, no!"

I dart on an interception course. Before I can reach the tottering girl, a dark-clad human shape dashes from between the same two chalets, clearly in pursuit, and snatches her up.

"Quick, into the 'Vi!" I beckon as the man turns. He takes two steps towards me—

"Freeze!" Zech's voice in my ear is soft—and iron.

My hand flies up towards the man, palm flat. "*Stay still!*" I barely murmur it, but I mouth it *very* clearly.

The man skids to a halt as those heavy footfalls grow louder—the only movement he makes is to fold both halves of his unzipped jacket over the child, enveloping her completely, and murmur something to her. Then he stands absolutely still, though the blood drains from his dark, dark skin, leaving it slightly grey-tinged.

From the slight *chink* sounds coming from my earpiece, Zech is swapping his rifle for the rex gun, which he took up there with him though he was really hoping not to have to use it. But he shouldn't need it. Not if we just stand still.

I maintain eye contact with the man as the ground shakes under our feet and the rex appears around the chalet just behind him, its head swiveling as it searches for that flash of un-raptor-like movement. Not that the rex won't make do with raptor, if one comes too close, so we don't need to worry about those feathered killers until it clears off.

Keeping my face calm and relaxed, I study the man to take my mind off the approaching carni'saur. Dressed all in black, he looks a few years older than Zech, mid-twenties, his tightly curling black hair close-cropped. Hmm, just visible over the jacket-wrapped little girl is a clerical collar. That's why he's all in black; he's a priest.

We're standing close enough together that I can see

the sweat on his face, his wide pupils... I go back to meeting his gaze and trying to look unconcerned. Something as tiny as eye contact can make a huge difference to someone trying not to break and run. Makes them feel they're not alone, and people can endure all manner of things if only they aren't alone. Even cityfolk.

Thud. Thud. Thud. The rex comes closer, still looking around, nostrils flaring. I'm not wearing any Scent-Blocker and for sure the other two aren't. If we stood in the middle of a field, that would be a big problem. But right here, in this human place surrounded by human scents, we won't stand out. *Right, Saint Des?*

The rex's head comes down, sniffing the front of the 'Vi, feet away from me, its distinctive carni'saur smell reaching my nostrils. A few scorch marks mar its otherwise smooth, healthy hide, and it's already growing quite a fine greenish-red display crest on top of its head, the only feathers retained by adult rex. From the way the priest's eyes widen, he's getting a good look at the beast. I try to hold his gaze, but he shuts his eyes tight. Praying, I guess. He still doesn't move, so that's fine.

Just don't let the little girl make a sound... Thank God he covered her head so she couldn't see. He's smart, for a city-man. Mebbe he can see Zech in the turret, pointing the rex gun. That should make him feel better, though if he knew how fast a rex can move when it feels like it...

Well. When the rex moves its head right close to me, sniffing, I add a few prayers of my own to his. I'm awfully tempted to shut my eyes as well, but I force myself to keep them open, taking in the details of a magnificent young animal I would never usually see so close-up. Though this is getting a little too close. Reeking rex breath overpowers every other scent. Sweat trickles down my forehead... The rex sniffs. Okay, *way* too close. If it sticks out that barely-mobile tongue and licks me, it'll *know* I'm prey. Okay and here's the tip of the tongue coming, the teeth inches away...

BANG!

The rex gun goes off like a small artillery piece. The rex leaps back and whirls, its tail smacking into the side of the 'Vi as it looks all around. I control a wince. How big's the dent? I won't be able to see that from here, but careful to move only my eyes, not my head, I locate a deep crater in the asphalt. Yes, a distraction shot only.

The rex turns in a circle several times, forcing both myself and the priest—whose eyes flew open at the shot—to crouch, unnoticed, to avoid the swinging tail. But soon enough it's stamping away, still looking around and making fretful sounds, on edge after that strange loud noise.

"Clear!" Zech's voice in my ear has never been so

welcome.

I dart forward, grab the man by the shoulders and hurry him to the 'Vi. The side door slides open as we reach it—*thanks, Zech*—and I boost him, girl still clutched in his arms, inside, then roll up and in myself. "Clear!"

The flash of movement I see in the distance even as the door hisses shut is surely a raptor. But the door's closed; it's been too slow. We're in.

Zech's rifle cracks, teaching the raptor manners, no doubt. Then his face appears in the turret hatch, glaring down at me where I still lie, panting, on the cool metal floor, the smell of incense tickling my nose after helping the priest in—incense and a hint of strawberry ice-cream from the girl. "What the heck was that, Isaiah? Have you lost your mind?"

I sit up, ignoring the fluttery feeling in my belly as the narrow escape makes itself felt. "It. Was. A. *Child!*"

"It was crazy!"

"Oh, shut up, Zech. If you'd been down here, you'd have done the same thing."

"Oh, yeah? *I* like being alive."

I get to my feet, swallowing another sharp retort. I musta scared him bad.

"You okay?" I ask the priest. So far he hasn't done anything other than sit and gasp and hug the child tight. His body's shaking, hard. His eyes move to mine—he's not totally frozen up, good—but he doesn't reply.

"We'd better stay clear of the rex until we're ready to lure it out," says Zech, abandoning his scolding in favor of more urgent matters. "We don't know how it will react next time it sees us."

Yeah, associating the 'Vi with the unpleasant noise, it may just walk away again—or it might attack us. Neither of us are stupid enough to think that any 'Vi is proof against a rex, let alone our rust-bucket. "Where'd it go?"

"Over the top of the hill."

"We've driven near most of the chalets this side," I say. "There's not so many over there and they know we're here. I guess that will have to do. They've heard the message."

"Yep. Let's move the 'Vi to the breach—discourage any more raptors coming in—and fish out the fence patch kit," says Zech. "No point luring the rex anywhere until we've got that ready."

"Right." I move towards the cab on legs that wobble just a fraction, but Zech slides down the turret ladder, landing lightly, and cuts me off.

"No, you look after your guests. I'll drive."

You brought them here; you deal with them, in other words. Zech's not the most social of guys. Especially when it comes to hysterical cityfolk and sobbing kids.

Not that the guy's exactly hysterical. And the girl's making only the tiniest, thinnest whimpering sound, probably because she's too scared to cry louder.

Since we don't have any whisky on board or anything like that, I fetch a slug of yesterday's cold coffee from the machine and put it in the priest's hand, guiding it to his mouth. "Here, drink this, down the hatch..."

He coughs as though it was whisky. "Phew, that's strong!"

"That's what happens when you let Zech make it, yeah. You okay, Father?"

"Uh, I guess. I seem to have all my limbs."

I laugh, relieved that he's getting it together so fast—and impressed.

"Hey, Mei Ling, you okay?" The priest unwraps the jacket at last, easing the child away from him. From the kid's delicately shaped eyes and black hair, she's got Chinese blood or something. Zech and I have so many races up our family tree we don't really look like anything. Chocolate mongrels, as Mom used to say, stroking our hair lovingly...

No. Not thinking about Mom now. I jerk my mind back to the little girl. "She okay?"

The girl clings tight, resisting his efforts to get a look at her, shivering like it's freezing outside.

"I don't think she's hurt. Just scared. Shhh, it's okay,

Mei Ling. It's okay. We're safe now. We're in the safest place in the resort, you know."

Hmm, deceptively easy to think that but even the chalets are more solid, if built to regulation, and we're the ones going up against the rex—and those three packs of feathered killing machines. This isn't where I'd choose to have a child right now.

I move to kneel beside Critter Cage One, at floor level, all six of its walls fully enclosed by solid reinforced steel. "Two-month-old leggy'saur" reads the display, and a red light glows. Unlocking the cage door, I slide it back, then beckon to the priest. "Come on, get her in here."

"What? I'm not putting her in *there*!"

"There are lights in there and a real cute little herbi'saur for her to cuddle." When the priest rises to his feet, still holding the girl, frowning and shaking his head, I add, "It's the safest place on the vehicle. We use it for our refuge. C'mon, she can play with Dinky, here."

A small downy head peers around the side of the cage door. Tiny claws hook around the edge. Large eyes blink. The nestling makes a cooing noise. Mei Ling turns her head to stare at it, her attention finally engaged. Whether her stare indicates fear or interest I'm not sure, but I grab a handful of seeds and hold them out to her. "Here, you can feed her. She likes these." I narrow my eyes slightly at Fr. Priest as Rexie roars in the distance, clearly recovering his aggression. *Just get her safe in there.*

He takes the hint and finally approaches, staggering slightly as Zech takes a corner too fast. Gently, he places his burden down inside the cage. "There we go, Mei Ling. All safe and sound. You play with Dinky for a while."

I put the seeds into her clutching hand, as she grabs at the withdrawing priest. "There, these are for Dinky. Look, she wants to be friends. Now, I've got to shut the door so she doesn't come out, okay? She can run really fast."

The little girl's mouth opens in a silent wail.

"It's okay, Mei Ling," says the priest, but I feel like a monster as I slide the door shut and lock it.

No wails from inside. Thank God she's not a wailer. Hopefully the cuddly-and-totally-harmless Dinky will distract her. "How old is she?"

"Uh...five?" He frowns at the unexpected question, but I just tap the nearby control pad, updating the cage display so it reads "Five-year-old human girl and two-month-old leggy'saur."

"Wh...?" For a moment I think he's going to ask why I took the time to do that, but then his mouth closes, lips thinning, and I'm pretty sure he's seeing the same thing as me—the 'Vi ripped open, adults all eaten, a little girl safe and unharmed in the refuge, but rescuers walking past, oblivious... Maybe I shoulda put her name, come to think. Oh well.

"Can you broadcast to the chalets that Mei Ling is safe?" asks the priest. "I'd hate for her parents to go out looking for her when I don't come back."

"Heck, yes!" I grab the console's Intercar mic.

I've just relayed the message when the 'Vi rolls to a halt and Zech appears in the cab doorway. "There's another pack of raptors eyeing up the breach," he announces. "Dakota. They must've smelled the human blood."

Raptors are so partial to human meat. This new pack are trespassing on the other pack's territory in hopes of bagging some. Tempting to let them in—then at least the Dakotaraptors will be too busy fighting each other to bother anyone—but every extra raptor inside the fence makes the clean-up more dangerous afterward. Another whole pack—not a good idea.

"I'm guessing they're thinking twice about it, now the 'Vi's here."

Zech bends to select a camera feed on the console. "Yep. The matriarch is nipping some silly juveniles that want to rush the breach anyway. Uh-huh, and now she's leading them all away."

Most matriarchs know what a 'Vi looks like—and what it means. They don't live long enough to reach that position in the pack if they don't. "I bet they'll lurk, though. We'd better keep the 'Vi here, if at all possible. You'd better stay, Zech, you're the better shot. I'll grab one of those resort trucks and some meat and lure the rex out through the main gates. I doubt it'll want to come near the breach again."

"Why not?" asks the priest. Huh, I still don't know his name.

"Painful memories." Zech smiles nastily. "Thousands of volts of 'em."

"Oh, of course. Can I, uh, help?"

"Mebbe you can come with me," I say. "One of us to fend raptors off the bait; one to drive."

Zech looks him up and down more doubtfully. "Can you fire a gun?"

"Yes. My aim's only middling, though."

"Middling's not much use," snorts Zech. "Know how fast raptors move?"

"So, how are you at driving?" I ask.

The priest smiles with confidence this time. "I did rally driving at regional level, before entering seminary."

"You did?" Huh, thanks, Saint Des! "Awesome, you can drive. Looks like I'm the bait guard. I'm Isaiah, by the way."

"Great name." White teeth gleam as the priest grins. "I'm Father Benedict, but most people call me Father

Ben."

"Hi, Father Ben. Grumpy, here, is my brother Zechariah."

"Hey, I've barely been out of bed for half an hour, and I missed breakfast."

"You've both got great biblical names. Are your parents religious?"

Zech's face goes blank, borderline hostile, as all his walls go up. "Our mom was, like, *holy*. Very. Our father just *thought* he was." He glances at me. "Fine, Father Ben can go with you, but speaking of, you're not going out there today with that whopping sin on you. I'll get the fence kit ready, you go in the cab with Father, here, and deal with that." His gaze returns to Father Ben. "You are a Catholic priest, right?"

"Yeah..." Father Ben eyes me, brows drawing together. "Is it true? You've got a mortal sin on your conscience?"

My cheeks burn so red-hot I could fry Zech a breakfast steak on one. I can't meet the young priest's eyes, only managing a hangdog nod, my heart accelerating as I wait for his response. My father would've... My whole body tenses, at the thought of what my father would've done, if he'd heard about this.

But the priest's voice comes calm and level. "Well, I'd certainly be very glad to take care of that for you."

I nod again, still unable to look at him, and lead the

way to the cab. Even though I'm kinda glad Zech mentioned it, 'cause I mighta been too embarrassed, I can't help throwing him a glare as I let the door slide closed behind me, but he shrugs it off unrepentantly.

"Oh, uh, here..." I shove Zech's sleeping bag to the side, making space, then sink into the driver's seat. My stomach flutters and churns worse than when the he-rex stuck its head in my face.

I shoot a glance at Father Ben. He's so much younger than most of the priests we see when we go to some city-church at Christmas or Easter—we've got a foolproof excuse not to go the rest of the time: too far from a Mass—but we know Mom can see us from heaven and would be so disappointed if we missed those special days. Not that we've got anything against God, really. Mom loved God. S'just the memories are too bad. Thanks to our father. Easier to talk to Saint Des and let *him* talk to the Father for us.

But after what I did at New Year, I've gotta face God, at least through this priest. I guess all priests are young at some point, they're just old for longer so I haven't seen many.

Father Ben smiles at me, his face still open and friendly, and my nerves ease a little. He's not looking at me differently now he knows I've done something really bad. I was afraid he would. My father would be laying his belt over my backside already, bare minimum.

I'm glad this priest's young, really. Feels more like talking to Jesus, rather than to the Father. Mom used to tell us Jesus was our big brother. Not that telling *Zech* about this was exactly easy, furious with worry as he was. At least Jesus/Father Ben hasn't just spent hours frantically wondering where I am and if I'm okay.

Glancing at Saint Des there on the dashboard, Father Ben says, "Shall we ask Saint Desmond to pray for us?"

I nod, so he murmurs a brief request for the saint's intercession, before going through the dimly remembered preliminaries of the Sacrament. I cross myself and wait nervously, but that done, he smiles at me again.

"Okay, we're in a rush, so just tell me about the big one. Just one, right?"

I nod yet again. A clattering from the living area says that Zech is excavating one of our storage lockers, trying to get to the rarely-used fence patch kit. I need to hurry up.

"Okay, um..." My voice comes out croaky and I clear my throat. "It was New Year's Eve. We were in-city. Parked at the 'Vi-park, as usual. Some of the other guys—they wanted to go to a bar. We...we don't usually, Zech and I. I only turned eighteen end of December and Zech don't like to drink. *Neither* of us really like drink. I even hate the *smell* of the stuff..." I

25

shudder. Just the thought of it...

...The smell of alcohol, already so strong, grows suffocating as the bottle smashes against the sink. I stumble backwards, doubled-over from the blow to my stomach, shrinking back as my father looms, the broken bottle in his hand. His free hand slams me back into the wall; the other brings the sharp glass edge to my throat...

"Isaiah? Are you all right?"

Cold sweat beads my face. I swallow hard, pushing the childhood memory away, and drag my thoughts together. "I'm okay. Sorry. Um, so, 'cause I'd turned eighteen, I kinda wanted to go to the bar, despite everything. Just once. I mean, not to get drunk or anything; just to have a couple of drinks. Felt a bit like, I dunno, I had to have gone once to be a grown-up, I guess." I rub my forehead wearily. It seems so *stupid*, now. If only the legal drinking age remained twenty-one, like in the old days, none of this would've happened. "It was dumb. But Zech agreed to go. And...and..."

Heat fills my cheeks again, chasing out the chillness. "I guess I broke Mom's fourth rule. Didn't mean to, but I did. And somehow that led to breaking the third rule, though I...I really don't remember any of it, to be honest."

Father Ben raises an eyebrow. "Mom's rules?"

"Oh, uh," I glance around and grab the framed list

from over Zech's bed. "Here. Our, um"—I swallow even harder—"our mom died when I was eight and Zech was eleven. He wrote down her...we call them her rules...so we wouldn't forget. 'Cause...our father would've *made* us forget."

I show him the list, watching as his eyes move down the familiar lines, Zech's best eleven-year-old handwriting, complete with some childish annotations from me, all faded by years of sun.

1) GOD LOVES YOU. DON'T FORGET.

(try to love Him even if He's called Father)

2) RESPECT EVERYTHING HE MADE.
(be nice to animals and everything.)

3) RESPECT WOMEN.

(why won't you tell Me what this Means, zech?)

4) RESPECT YOURSELF.
(no drinking or unHealtHy stuFF.)

5) NO SWEARING.

(saint des doesn't Like it. Nor MoM.)

6) NO LYING, STEALING OR BAD STUFF.
(so No bulLying or Murdering PeoPLe, either.)

7) Safety Catch, Safety Catch, Safety Catch!

"Okay, Mister Wilson added number seven," I add, flushing. "There's, um, a story behind that. He used to own this 'Vi. We worked for him for years, until he retired."

"I see. So, ah..."

"Oh, yeah, so Zech did explain number three years ago. But I ended up drunk, so there went number four, and then..." I grind to a halt again, my throat tight. "I woke up in some apartment in the city and I'd obviously broken number three."

I swallow, once again assaulted by that raw, tearing sense of...of loss. I had something precious and I just threw it away in the mud, like it was nothing. I don't even *remember*. "I-I'm really sorry." My eyes sting, but I refuse to cry. "I'm really, *really* sorry. I just wish I could, could wind things back and…do them over. But…but I can't. And I feel so *dirty*..."

"I know," says Father Ben softly, eyes filled with concern. Not anger. "I know. Now, I have to ask, the young lady, she was happy about all this? She didn't seem...mad at you?"

I frown. I'd never thought about it in quite those terms. "Uh...she wasn't that young, really. And she..." Even more heat creeps into my cheeks. I don't want to say, but this is confession. I have to be honest. "Um, she kinda laughed at me. Teased me, y'know. But she offered me breakfast, though I felt too awful to eat much. Wanted to swap numbers in case I was in-city again. I never entered her number on our 'Vi system, though. Threw the paper away."

"Huh." Father Ben's brows draw together darkly and he speaks almost under his breath. "Maybe I'm asking the wrong person."

"What d'you mean? You saying..." I thought I couldn't blush any more, but I was wrong. "Saying she, uh, like, took advantage of me?"

"What, the thought never crossed your mind?"

I look at the floor, cheeks super-heating. Okay, so I have wondered any number of times why she took me home when I was clearly so drunk. And so much younger. Wished she hadn't. Wished it over and over. It's not like she seemed to have so much of a headache in the morning. Not like mine. And it feels like Father Ben's more mad at her than at me.

"That's what happened, anyway," I mutter.

"Okay. Well, casting aside your precious free will by getting drunk intentionally is certainly a mortal sin, but since it happened by accident none of it is quite as bad as that. So you didn't actually..."

Thud-thud. Zech bangs on the door. "Are you done yet? The kit's all ready. People to save; hurry it up."

"Right, never mind." Father Ben dismisses the rest of what he was saying with a wave of his hand. "Just remember, people always assume it's the guy's fault. But sometimes, it actually isn't. Now, for your penance—you can do it later—say..."

"Not *Our Fathers*, please..." The words squeeze out before I can stop them, though his previous words are burrowing into my mind, strange and tantalizing.

Father Ben looks at me for a long moment, like there's a million questions—a million conversations—he'd like to have with me, but of course there's no time. "Okay, you know the chaplet of Saint Desmond?"

"Yes." Every hunter knows that one, Catholic or not. There's not a lot of words to it, either. "Jesus, I trust in You," is most of it.

"Say that every day for a week, for, er, for good judgment and strength of will. Okay, just tell me you're sorry, and I'll absolve you. I know you *are*, but just for the record, as it were."

I squint at the air beside his head, picturing some sort of recording angel taking notes, and mumble the necessary words.

"I absolve you in the name of the Father and of the Son and of the Holy Spirit. Right, you're squeaky clean and ready to be eaten by raptors."

I splutter, then laugh so hard I have to clutch my rib cage. "And what about you?" I demand at last.

He grins. "Not that long since I went to confession. I'll take my chances."

I grin back. "You're a real cool customer, for a city-man. You know this is pretty dangerous, right?"

"I'd figured that out, yes. People to save, right?"

"Yeah. Let's go, then."

Soon Father Ben and I stand by the side door, waiting for Zech to give us the all clear. His rifle's been barking regularly the whole time I've been getting us ready. Hopefully a lot of the rash juveniles are dead by now or getting wary. We're both slathered in ScentBlock cream, which will help protect us from the rex, but it's not totally scentless itself, so it doesn't work well on raptors. They tend to figure out humans come with that scent. I'm not convinced it's totally hiding the incense but no carni'saur will know what to make of *that*.

"Clear." Zech's voice speaks in my best earpiece. My second best one is currently in Father's Ben's ear.

"Come on." I hit the "open" button and jump to the ground. The priest hesitates only a split second before dropping down beside me.

The door hisses shut and I start running, aiming for the resort truck parked outside the utility hut at the end of the nearest row of chalets. I've got my rifle in my hands but I focus most on speed. I can hear Father Ben following, carrying the sealed pack of meat, a spare rifle over his shoulder in case we end up cornered somewhere, loaded—just like mine—with safety rounds that won't go through the chalet walls.

I'm within twenty feet of the truck—well in range—when a juvenile Utahraptor—the very largest species—leaps onto the truck roof, all but licking its lips as it bunches its legs to spring. I keep on sprinting. By the time I've raised my gun, Zech will...

Crack.

Yep, Silly Juvenile collapses on the truck roof, twitching claws perilously close to the door I'm aiming for.

Crack-crack.

Zech takes care of that concern with a double-tap to its head, so I ignore the feathery body and yank the passenger door open. "In!"

Father Ben dives inside without needing a second invitation, straight over into the driver's seat, and I leap in beside him.

By the time I've slammed the door, he's wedged my spare rifle in the middle and pulled the sun visor down—the keys tumble into his lap. He rams them straight into the ignition and turns them—I breathe a sigh of relief as the engine starts first time, but I frown as I look around. Although it's a truck, it's got no window grilles or wheel shields or anything. Completely naked, a city-style vehicle like something out of a video from the early twenty-first century. Great.

We knew that before we left the 'Vi, but there was nothing else close enough. Since we're not planning to stop, it really shouldn't matter all that much.

"Clip as many raptors as you have to," I say quickly. "But *don't* ram them straight on. *Clip them*. If we lose the engine, we die."

He nods and we move forward. "Up the hill?"

"Yep, up and over. I think Rexie's on the far side somewhere. Come on, speed is our best defense."

Father Ben obliges, and a few moments later we're tearing up the hill at sixty...seventy...miles per hour, chalets and leathery raptor faces a blur as we pass them. I try not to hang onto my door handle too noticeably.

"What are you even doing here, anyway?" The question pops out.

"Stopping overnight with a parish group on the way back from a diocesan pilgrimage to the shrine of Our Lady of Speedy Succor," he grunts, taking a corner without hardly slowing down.

"Oh." I try not to close my eyes as we zoom between two chalets. "Where you from, then?"

"Exception State." The wheel turns, we straighten up again. He seems happy to talk and drive, even at this speed. Mebbe it's taking his mind off his nerves.

Exception is one state away, fairly northern-central, and I've never been there. "Oh, I've heard it has a nice climate." I try to watch for raptors but we're going so fast it's impossible—and probably unnecessary.

"Yeah, it does."

"Not many cities, though. Some of the guys seem to think that's a bad thing, but sounds nice to me."

"Not many, no. Maybe that's why they seem to have trouble attracting enough hunters to the state. Though where doesn't struggle with that?"

I laugh—nervously. We've just spun on one wheel—so it seems—and shot between yet another pair of chalets, making a frightened velociraptor leap to one side. Father Ben seems to know where he's going, anyway.

"Exception City recently revamped the 'Vi-park," Father Ben adds. "They put in a fire pit and a shelter so you guys can have, like, cook-outs there and stuff. Spent quite a few dollars on it."

"Guess they really are short of hunters," I say. Most 'Vi-parks are little more than grass-tufted stretches of asphalt with a tap and a waste facility, poked away in some run-down corner of the city, 'least, they are here in Rado State.

"It seems so. I was assistant priest in the nearest city parish when they did it and it seemed to go down well with your guys. Never much for turning up at church, your lot, but if I went down to the 'Vi-park, well, they put my city parishioners to shame, that's for sure. Lined up for confession, turned out for the Mass, then filled me up with food and drink until I could barely drive home."

"That was to make sure you'd be back," I said dryly. "Where are you now?"

"A smaller city, near… Whoa!" He brings us to a rapid halt as we come out onto the top of an extensive, manicured slope and see Rexie lower down, sniffing at some picnic tables.

"Okay, target acquired," I murmur, speaking more to Zech, then I turn to Father Ben again. "I'm going to chuck the meat in the back, soon as it's in there, we need to get under Rexie's nose, okay, before the raptors can get it? And as soon as he's interested, we head for the main gate, making sure not to lose him. But *don't* let him catch us. Even small as he is, if he takes hold of this little vehicle, he could flip us, easy as anything."

"I've got it." Father Ben's gone a little grey around the edges again, staring downslope at the young T. rex, his knuckles pale as he grips the wheel. "You just…" he clears his throat. "You just keep the raptors off us."

"I'll do my best." I'm busy cutting open the meat packet and opening the sun roof—the dead juvenile slid off several corners ago. "Just remember there're no grilles on this thing and I'll need to be back inside once the rex gets interested, which will limit my line of fire, so be ready to duck if something gets past me. Okay, ready?"

"Ready. *Holy Mother, Guardian Angels, pray for us. Lord, save us. Oh yeah, Saint Desmond, pray for us...*"

"*Amen!*" I pop up from the sun roof, hefting the meat into the open back of the truck, making sure to touch only the plastic wrapping to avoid getting meat juices on me, then I wedge my feet as well as I can, one on the dash, trying to achieve the best arc of movement. I slap the roof. "Go!"

We move downslope towards the rex, but we've barely travelled thirty feet before a Dakotaraptor leaps into the truck and grabs at the meat. I aim for it, but the wily old creature leaps straight out again, a hunk in its mouth, and whisks away. I shoot a younger, slower one as it makes too leisurely an approach, then duck back into the cab as an older one lands near the rim of the sun roof, deadly toe-claw slicing through the roof. My bullet goes through the roof just as easily and leaves it screeching on the grass behind us, but when I emerge again no fewer than six dog-sized velociraptors are in the back, gulping meat as fast as they can tear it off.

"Get out of there!" I shoot one and it topples out—the rest scatter. The hunk of meat, the largest we could carry and already quite small to tempt a rex, looks very depleted. "Argh, you vermin!"

Now we're further down the slope, away from the buildings, I've got more time to see them coming and it's easier to keep them off, but three large Utahraptors rushing in at once send me into the cab again, and when I'm able to straighten up, those cheeky velociraptors are back. "Clear *off!*"

My heart sinks as they scatter again. Little remains of the meat but a smeary plastic wrapper. Is the rex going to be interested? It's stomping up to take a look, so we'll soon know. I slide quietly back into the cab and peep out.

"Wait..." I whisper to Father Ben, as the huge head comes down over the back of the truck. With so little bait left, we need to let it get the scent properly.

But, nostrils flaring, the beast—did it just *yawn?*—turns and ambles away.

"Heck! It's not hungry." Has it eaten someone? My heart plummets. If it has, it's not suitable for release and we need the rex gun. No, there's no fresh blood around its teeth or face. It's simply eaten fairly recently, is all.

"What do we do?" Without me telling him, Father Ben reverses gently after the rex, taking advantage of its raptor-deterring presence and giving it the option of changing its mind.

I swallow. Zech's not going to like this. "We appeal to its hunting instincts. Let's try this again. Get ready."

"What are you doing, Isaiah?" Zech's voice growls in my ear.

"Just luring the rex, Zech, as planned." I whip my hunting knife from my belt and draw the blade across the back of my left arm, making Father Ben's eyes widen. *Ouch.* Bright blood wells from the cut, the scent filling the cab. ScentBlock cream problem overcome. "Get ready, Father." I stand again and wave my bloody arm. Wave both arms. Yell. "Hey, dino prince, look here! Smell this. Over here, you silly beast…"

The young rex swivels, nostrils flaring, eyes immediately drawn to the movement. Yep, nothing like the smell of fresh blood, is there?

No, there isn't. Leathery raptor faces pop around every chalet and tree in sight, feathered ruffs bushing out eagerly. The rex's more mobile crest rises high as it turns and heads our way. Gathering speed. Breaking into a run.

I slap the roof. "*Go!*"

I try to wedge myself more firmly against the edge of the sun roof as we accelerate rapidly up the hill. The rex lengthens its stride to a full-out sprint. "No faster, that's its top speed," I call to Father Ben.

I wave my arms at the rex some more, to keep its interest, then grab my rifle in a two-handed grip again as we reach the chalets. Some of the raptors have flitted away from the approaching colossus, but some remain, eyes on me.

Soon one leaps for the truck. It's a poorly aimed jump and I'm able to simply duck to the side, nothing but a whiff of deadly raptor scent reaching me as the young Dakotaraptor tumbles on the asphalt, feathers flying. It rolls onto its feet and darts away, Rexie's teeth snapping closed a few inches from the tip of its feathery tail.

"Keep away from the chalets as much as possible!" I yell. "I need to see them coming!"

Oh no, why's he...? Father Ben's just spun the wheel—I cling on one-handed, the other holding my rifle in a death grip—and aimed us into the gap between two chalets. Did he mishear me?

Argh! I drop back flat on the roof as a raptor plummets towards me, getting my gun up just in time...*crack!* The raptor jerks in midair and topples onto the hood with a crash. We only swerve slightly before it falls off, but I yell, "Sorry!"

As we come out onto another of the little inter-chalet roads, I draw breath to tell Father Ben again to stay out in the open—if he can find any "open"—but before I can, Father Ben two-wheels us around an ornamental fountain—Rexie smashes straight through it, crest feathers near-vertical now with the excitement of the chase—and suddenly we're on the much wider main driveway down through the resort to the gate, thank God. I guess he did hear me, after all.

Raptors flit from chalet to chalet, hiding from Rexie and from my rifle, just waiting for an opportunity. Blood runs down my arm, hot and sticky. I'm officially the tastiest snack in a fifty-mile radius. I'm in view of the 'Vi, too.

"You okay, Isaiah? I see blood."

"Fine, Zech. Is that guard ready on the gate controls?"

"Yep. Just tell me when. Why aren't you inside the truck?"

"Stop distracting the bait, Zech."

I take a shot at a raptor that's showing too much of itself and hit it, making the others draw back a little.

Rexie tosses his head. His eyes remain on me, but he's breathing heavily. T. rex don't usually go in for long pursuits. "Ease up a bit, Father Ben. We're wearing our boy out."

Slowing down is the last thing I really want to do, since it leaves us far more vulnerable to the feathered menace, but if Rexie loses interest and stops following we'll have done all this for nothing.

The truck slows a little. Rexie flares his crest and steps out more eagerly. That's it. Chalets rush past; not far to the gate now.

Five velociraptors streak from behind a fence and leap up at me. I drop down into the cab, slamming the sun roof—crash, a sharp little claw breaks it at once. Shrugging glass off my shoulders, I put five or six shots through the roof, then fling open the empty window frame, snapping on my safety catch for a moment to reverse my rifle and club the last velociraptor in the jaw. It tumbles off, screeching, and gets stepped on by Rexie. For a moment, the T. rex hesitates, head lowering, turning back towards the fresh meat.

"Hey!" I squeeze the cut—*ow*—and wave my arms like a maniac. "Hey, what do you want with a tiny mouthful of feathery raptor? Look here! I'm all pink and featherless and soft, no horns, no tough hide, look how tasty I am..."

Rexie forgets the velociraptor meat behind him and powers forward again with renewed determination. His teeth get awfully close before Father Ben accelerates. But the tired beast's not going to follow for much longer.

I throw a glance over my shoulder. There's the gate. Will Rexie approach the fence after what happened this morning?

"Zech, get the gates open. Father Ben..." I swallow. "Slow down. We need him really close. Like, *really* close." He mustn't be thinking about anything further away than the meal a few feet from the end of his nose.

As soon as the gates are open, Father Ben slows down. Rexie gets closer. And closer. I'm sweating again, washing my ScentBlocker off, no doubt.

Rexie's head moves slightly, his eyes shift to the side...looking at the fence? "Slower!"

His attention flicks back to me as I draw closer. He's

coming alongside, now, stretching over the truck-bed, trying to reach me. I extend my rifle carefully, ready to fend his head away—or try. "Hold us steady," I croak.

Rexie puts on a burst of speed, grabbing for me, but he's too tired, and a touch of the accelerator from Father Ben thwarts him...

And then we're through the gates. "Father Ben, go! Zech, close the gates!"

Father Ben accelerates, full throttle, leaving the disappointed he-rex behind in moments.

Phew. So that's the rex dealt with. I drop back into the cab, placing my rifle on the seat. It's probably safer out here than inside the resort fence, just at the moment. All the same... "Keep up the speed," I warn Father Ben. "Remember that second pack of Dakotaraptors are around somewhere and this vehicle is naked." With no grilles, the broken sun roof hardly makes any difference.

I pull an emergency dressing pack from my ammo sash, rip it open and mop my arm with the odor control wipe. Then I clap a handful of clotting crystals onto the wound and plaster the wodge of artificial skin over the top, pressing down all the edges carefully to seal in scent. One more swipe with the odor wipe and I toss it up through the broken roof window. I wouldn't usually litter, but it is biodegradable, so under the circumstances... I press another odor neutralizing wipe to the bloodstains on my pants, for what it's worth, then chuck it after the other one.

"Right, let's get to the 'Vi. Where's Rexie gone?"

Father Ben's been keeping an eye on the beast in his mirrors.

"Sulking near the gate." Father Ben turns and heads back that way. "Can we drive past him?"

"If we time it right, yeah, he's so tired now. By which I mean, if we go really fast. Doesn't seem like that'll be a problem for you."

A grin crosses the priest's tense face.

"Zech? You can see us, right?"

"Yep."

"Tell the guard when to open the gates, then. Okay?"

"Okay."

"Floor it, Father."

The weary rex stares at us as we tear towards it, making a half-hearted lurch in our direction as we come close—which Father Ben evades easily, though the maneuver makes my empty stomach churn. It pursues for a few paces, then sees the fence ahead and stops dead, glaring after us as we disappear through the gates, but making no attempt to follow. Yep, that's one rex that'll be staying away from fences from now on. Good.

Father Ben doesn't slow down once we're inside,

thank God. "Get as near to the 'Vi as you can," I tell him, though I doubt I need to.

He screeches to a halt so close we're able to slide out and jump straight up through the side door, which Zech opens from the turret. By the time we've got the door shut, Zech's already taken a shot at an interested raptor.

Giggles, coos, and childish chatter come from Critter Cage One—clearly Dinky and Mei Ling have taken to each other—so we climb straight up into the turret to join Zech.

Zech glowers at my cut arm but just says, "We need to get that fence fixed, and I'd better do it since you're bleeding. But there're a horrible lot of raptors around."

"D'you think that guard could get his butt over here and help? It's his job."

"I've not managed to talk him out of his booth yet, though that's a proper outSPARK vehicle he's got parked there, with a full complement of heavy duty window grilles."

A poor design, though. No roof window to shoot from, so no use for luring the rex, even if it had been parked closer.

"We'd better get him here somehow or, even with Father Ben's help, this is going to be way too risky."

"Let me speak to him." Father Ben picks up the turret's Intercar mic. "Hello. Trevor, isn't it?"

"Who's this?"

"Father Benedict. We chatted a bit last night, remember?"

"Oh, right, the black dude."

"That's right, the black dude." Father Ben's voice is a little dry, but he seems unfazed. "It's nice to know you're okay; you were one of the people I was most concerned about when it became clear what was going on."

"You were?"

"Of course. It's the fence guard's job to deal with this sort of situation, right?"

"Uh, yeah. Of course."

"Well, the hunters have got the rex outside. Now they need to patch the fence. If they get eaten while trying to do it, I guess it'll all be up to you again. But if you pop over and help provide cover, things will be sorted out in no time."

A long silence. Lip curling, Zech opens his mouth, but Father Ben shakes his head, silencing him.

"I'm not hunting no raptors on foot," replies Trevor at last, his voice shaking.

"Heaven forbid," says Father Ben. "No one will be doing *that*, I hope."

Zech catches my eye and smiles sourly. Yeah, odds are someone will be in the end and it'll be us. But we're not doing it for free, so we'll worry about that later.

"Can you even cover me from right over there?"

Trevor...whines.

Since Zech still looks too peeved to speak nicely, I say, "Yeah, we can see the booth clearly; it's in range."

The turret's glass windows are already raised, so I lift my rifle and aim it the right way, checking the tip is between the bars. Zech raises his own and Father Ben, after cocking his head to watch exactly what we're doing, does the same. I glance to make sure that his muzzle is through the bars and unimpeded, catching Zech looking too. We don't want any ricochets.

"You're covered," says Father Ben. "Three guns, so move to the vehicle as soon as you like."

Three guns, but whether Father Ben can hit anything at such long range is a question there's no need to trouble Trevor with. Even Zech or I might miss a shot at this distance, but Trevor's only darting to his truck—parked right outside—and with the good visibility around the fence booth, he barely needs cover at all.

After several long moments—does Father Ben need to talk him around some more?—the door of the gate booth opens and a figure darts out and flings itself inside the truck. The engine starts. Here he comes. He pulls up beside the rear door. I push the button to open it as he leaps out. And...closed. We've acquired an extra gun to cover Zech while he works on the fence. Good. Three's a bit more like it.

Zech goes below, relieving Trevor of the fence's security fob, quizzing him on what his rifle's loaded with—safety rounds, good—and sending him on up with—ah, bless you, brother—an emergency box of city-bought snack bars. From the way Father Ben bites into his, he's had no breakfast either. Trevor refuses one and simply stands clutching his rifle, looking queasy and awkward. He couldn't possibly have got the job if he wasn't a good shot; let's just hope he can aim well under pressure.

After pulling on heavy rubber boots—to help protect against any mistake with the electricity—and a heavy leather tunic—designed to protect against the tiny, deadly-in-large-numbers piranha'saurs of which there is currently no sign, but also providing some protection from dog-sized velociraptors—Zech passes a load of extra ammo up to us in the turret.

"I'm setting the movement sensor now." I tap the turret console screen, selecting the area beyond the fence and arming the sensor. If anything comes from that direction, we'll get a warning. We can concentrate on the teeming resort side. "Okay, it's set."

"Good." Zech gathers the patching equipment and lets himself out the side nearest to the fence.

"Keep your eyes open," I tell Father Ben and Trevor, raising my rifle again—they do the same. "Nothing gets past us, okay?"

"Nothing," agrees Father Ben, though he's sweating worse now than when he was out there driving. I can smell it even through what's left of his cream. I guess shooting really isn't his best skill.

"If one breaks cover and attacks," I add, "don't just leave it to me. Both of you try and hit it too, okay? I'll probably bring it down, but anyone can miss a raptor if it leaps just as they fire."

Father Ben nods; Trevor just gulps. I fight back a surge of resentment. Zech's out there doing *his* job for him. Not that there's any point waiting for Trevor to do it, that's clear enough. And it's not like we won't get well paid for this day's work, eventually. We can claim a bounty on each dead raptor from DAPdep, along with a rex management fee, and the resort owners are expected to chip in too. Not that either of us would do today's work just for money, mind you, however much we want that new 'Vi. We're not that mad or that greedy.

I keep ninety-nine percent of my attention on anywhere raptors can come from, stealing the odd glance at the screen on the console ledge that displays the camera feed from Zech's side of the 'Vi. Yep, Zech's almost up to the fence already, walking with his eyes on the ground as he watches for stray wires. The boots should help if he steps on one, but with that sort of voltage it's better not to take chances.

Another glance... He's reached the nearest fence post with a control box, where he'll use Trevor's security fob to switch off the power in the breached section and both neighboring sections. The fence is up-to-date enough to have a buried "live" cable, electrifying each section separately, so that a breach doesn't power down the whole thing.

Will the resort fit an even more up-to-date double fence, after this? They're more affordable than they were and getting fairly common on farms. Rex still go through them—once shocked and running they're hard to stop—but the inner fence has been known to turn them back, sometimes.

An adult raptor peeks out at Zech, eyes the 'Vi — and whips back out of sight before I can line up the sights on its head.

Working swiftly, no messing around, Zech pulls the wire clippers from the patch kit and extends the telescopic handles, then sets to work clipping away any of the broken wires that will obstruct the repair.

A juvenile raptor peers around one of the more distant chalets, now, staring at Zech greedily.

"Take a shot at it, Father Ben?" Good practice for him while the stakes aren't high. If he misses and it attacks instead of running—hardly likely—we've got several hundred feet in which to hit it.

Father Ben moistens his lips, adjusts his position. I

check his muzzle again—still through the bars, good. Finally...*crack!*

The raptor screeches in terror and bolts back in among the buildings.

"Sorry," mutters the priest.

"No, the range was quite long. That was a good shot. Just very low, the bullet ruffled its underfeathers. Compensate, and you should nail the next one."

Father Ben relaxes a little.

It's a reasonable distance from the closest chalets to the fence, and even the juveniles sense danger. A lot of faces peer out and then disappear before we can fire. Finally, another juvenile takes its time eyeing Zech, and Father Ben puts a bullet in its chest.

"Great shot." I put a mercy-round into the twitching creature's head and throw Father Ben a smile, though my eyes never quite leave the scene in front of me. "We can get the claws for you, later. You can start a claw necklace." Hunters—farmers, too—string raptors' big killing claws on necklaces as a silent proclamation of their hunting skills.

Father Ben laughs weakly. "I don't think they'll go with my vestments."

I shrug. "Suit yourself. Zech and I can sell them, otherwise." Farmers tend to collect all their claws, but like most hunters, Zech and I sell our spares, keeping only the very finest to wear—raptor claws having no scarcity value as far as we're concerned.

Zech's finished clipping the wires from the opposite fence post now and is busy taking out the wire spools and extending the pincers, ready to attach the temporary wires. He's getting on well.

I raise my eyes from the screen to see a juvenile Utahraptor leap over a chalet's flowerbed, sprinting flat-out towards the fence—and Zech—on strong three-toed feet, killing claws raised clear of the earth.

I begin adjusting my aim—Trevor's gun barks, the shot puffing up soil very close to the raptor—I aim for the body, not head, of this fast-moving target—Father Ben tries too, his shot falling too far behind—I track the raptor for another half-second until I'm sure...squeeze... *Crack!* The raptor jerks, stumbles forward, falls, thrashes weakly. *Crack.* A bullet in its head ends its suffering.

"You need to factor in the speed," I tell Father Ben, as the build-up of gun-smoke makes Trevor sneeze. "Your shot was well behind it. Height was good, though. I'd say practice will make perfect, but right now, I'd rather you didn't get any more."

"Too right," says Father Ben fervently. "Your brother must feel like he's lying on a platter with an apple in his mouth."

"No, because we're up here."

"Because *you're* up here. I'm not much help with this."

"Oh, you are. Raptors can distinguish between one and more. And they recognize guns. The older, smarter ones do. That's why hardly any of them are bothering us and only juveniles. If it was just me up here, it would be a bloodbath. I could probably keep them off Zech if it all went right but one jammed round and he'd've had it. Super risky."

I don't glance at Trevor, but I do speak to him. "So, Trevor, who's likely to be coming to help? Any farmers?" It's a wild area, no doubt why this scenic resort is here, and I don't recall any farms for miles.

"I doubt it. They're all so far away."

"So, what are the procedures for something like this happening?"

"This isn't supposed to *happen*! I check the fence three times a day, make any minor repairs. The maintenance guys come once a month; it's kept in really good order. I guess management will get them out to fix this hole, but I don't know what they're going to do about all these raptors."

"Rex have gone through *city* fences before now. Surely you have a breach procedure?"

"Sure, everyone go inside and stay there. I made all the broadcasts and everything."

I frown, watching a velociraptor peering through the undergrowth in another chalet garden. "Go inside and stay and wait for *what*? Once you've got a breach, it's not going to fix itself. So, who is coming to deal with it?"

"Dunno," comes the sheepish mutter. "I called head office and told them, and I bet every member of staff did too, but they said they'd get back to me. I let them know when you guys showed up, but I haven't heard any more."

"If they haven't planned for this, are they going to try to declare it out-of-control and make the SPARK Brigade come out?" The government passed a law a long, long time ago that breaches on private land were the landowner's responsibility, back when they got too fed up with people not maintaining their fences and just relying on the SPARKies to rush to their rescue. To get them out now, you have to have no other option and there are heavy penalties.

"*No way*. There'd be a *huge* fine. I guess they'll send someone."

I keep myself from rolling my eyes only because I don't want to leave Zech uncovered while I do it. Though I'm starting to suspect we may be in line for a juicy contract, here. "Do you want to bag that little velociraptor, Father Ben?"

"*That's* a threat to Zechariah?" Father Ben sounds startled.

"Not to Zech on its own or not much, but every last one of these critters is going to have to be dealt with."

Mebbe the priest is uncomfortable with shooting it when it's not right-this-moment threatening someone. "Don't worry, I've got it."

Crack. One less. Only another dozen or so to go. This could be a long day. With that in mind, I stop grilling Trevor about the resort's inadequate breach arrangements and start picking off as many raptors as I possibly can. It has the added advantage of seriously deterring them from trying for Zech, who's got quite a few wires fixed over the gap now. He'll be able to put the fence sections back on soon and return to the 'Vi.

Ping.

The turret console chimes. Either Zech or I have a message. I'm not looking now. There's a raptor much further up the hill, almost out of range but standing nice and still. I rest the end of my rifle on the bars to steady it and take my time aiming. *Crack.* Got it. How many more?

The communicator at Trevor's belt bleeps. He reaches for it—

"Hey, *leave* it!" I protest.

"But..."

"Call them back when Zech's inside! It won't be long now."

He mutters something cross under his breath involving "dirty dog," which is about the stupidest of a whole list of dumb city insults commonly hurled at hunters. A dirty hunter is a dead hunter, quick enough—like cats, we're constantly washing ourselves, our clothes, and our vehicles in order to avoid notice by larger predators. Cityfolk, now they *always* stink of something or other.

I ignore him. Honestly, I'm quite easy-going, but this guy is getting on my nerves. If he'd just had the guts to get in his truck and drive up and down, looking like he was in control of the situation, people wouldn't have panicked and practically everyone—maybe even everyone—would be alive. And now he'd rather answer his phone than protect the guy who's doing his job for him? *Saint Des, give me patience!* Zech would probably eviscerate him if he knew—at least verbally.

Hah, Zech's packed the kit away and is moving to the fence control panel. And the next time I look, he's jogging back towards the 'Vi. I fix my attention to the danger spots, since the closer Zech gets, the more likely an attack. But I must've scared the raptors enough because nothing tries for him, and then the door hisses closed below us and he's safe again. I let out a long breath.

"Fence is back up," calls Zech. "Piece of cake. Speaking of, did you leave any of those bars?"

"You hunters are all crazy," mutters Trevor, reaching for his communicator.

"*That* was your job, in case you didn't realize." I bite

back further words with effort. If he can't work out that there're a lot of needless deaths on his useless shoulders, I guess I don't want to be the one to point it out. The coward might off himself or anything. Though, even if the owners don't end up declaring it out-of-control, there's bound to be some sort of inquiry, and they'll probably hang this wimp out to dry.

Kicking off the heavy boots and shedding the tunic, Zech climbs up to join us as Trevor checks who called him.

"Here." I rip open a bar and give it to Zech.

"Breakfast, finally." He bites into it, speaking with his mouth full. "The patch isn't piranha'saur-proof, of course, but it should keep out velociraptors and up. So, who's coming to deal with all this?"

I shrug. "I asked. He doesn't know."

Trevor makes *shhhh* noises, holding the phone to his ear. "Hello? Yes, it's Trevor Lane. Yes, the fence guard. Sorry, sir, I was— No, that's not an error, we have restored peripheral integrity. No, sir, the hunters did... Yes, they expelled the T. rex prior to that. *Who, me?* Uh, there're an awful lot of raptors still in here, sir. Er..." He shoots me an urgent look and mouths *how many?*

I shrug again. "I'd say somewhere between twelve and twenty. Awfully big packs in these wild areas."

In farming areas raptor packs may be no more than five to seven individuals, varying a bit with species, but out here, packs of ten or even more are common.

"...Might be twenty raptors still inside the perimeter, sir. Are you sending someone to— Yes, yes, they're right here. Yes, sir."

He holds the phone out to about half-way between Zech and me. "It's the director. He wants to talk to you guys."

Zech takes the phone, swallowing his last bite of bar. Yep, this looks familiar. We're about to be hired to clean up this mess, and it's going to take a while. But we'll get a fat paycheck we can put towards our new 'Vi.

"I'll get some food," I mutter to Zech and slide down the ladder.

Father Ben follows me, opening Critter Cage One to check on the little girl. She accepts a snack bar happily but resists any attempt to get her out, either too scared of what might be outside or too reluctant to leave her new playmate, with whom she's cheerfully splitting the bar when Father Ben shuts the door again.

After setting out a few of our folding chairs around the drop-down table, I make a big stack of cheese sandwiches super-fast—a quick smear of lard, a hunk of cheese—and bite into one. Father Ben accepts another, and I take one up to Zech.

"Quite frankly, that offer is pathetic," he's saying, when I stick my head into the turret. "That the sort of value you put on your own life, is it? Why don't you go get a quote from one of those big city companies with all the latest gadgets? See what they'd charge for putting down twenty raptors in an inhabited area, huh? Or just declare it out-of-control. *That'll* be cheaper, you think?"

I share an eye roll with him and go below again. His voice drifts after me, now a little muffled by a mouthful of sandwich. "Two sweeps of the resort to put the raptors down. At least. Then we evacuate everyone. Then we do another sweep, *on foot*, to find the one napping somewhere that got missed, before the police and coroners and fence repair teams can come on site and start work. Then we provide cover while they fix the fence, say two days, most likely—this isn't some tiny culling operation we're talking about here..."

"Why the heck are these people always so stingy?" I say to Father Ben, as I lean over the console to see who that message is for. "We're no rip-off merchants."

"Human nature?"

"Yeah, I guess." The message is for me, from an unrecognized number.

"Did you hear about those cheesed off hunters up north?" Father Ben says. "They put a live velociraptor in a soundproofed box and shipped it to a client they were having a payment dispute with."

I laugh. "Zech and I haven't got that mad at anyone

yet."

"Good thing too. The thing bit half the guy's face off, then chased his wife around the apartment until she beat its brains out with a frying pan."

I whistle. "She did? That's good going for a city-lady."

"The guy was agitating for a charge of attempted murder. The hunters claimed they meant it as a prank and hadn't intended him to end up with seventy-two stitches and three rounds of plastic surgery and I guess they probably hadn't, but it was clear they were going to go down for a good long stretch. No one ever gives you guys the benefit of the doubt."

"Hang on, I did hear about this. They asked everyone to chip in to get the bail money together, then they skipped off into the neighboring state, right?"

States are so keen on their autonomy and so resistant to federal interference these days that you've gotta actually kill someone before you'll get extradited across a state boundary. Changing states will deal with a whole lotta problems, as Mister Wilson understood very well. Of course, that's not as easy as it sounds if you're trapped inside a city when relocating becomes necessary.

"That's right. So you think their friends knew they'd lose their money?"

"Heck, yeah. I bet they're working hard and paying

the other guys back as fast as they can now, though."

"Hunters stick together, huh?"

"Usually, yeah. You just said it; no one else sticks up for us."

Turning my attention back to the console, I open the message.

I need you to send me $500.

I snort and hit *delete*. I don't usually get much spam because I'm not online much, but I know it when I see it.

"That's our final offer," Zech's saying, using his bored voice again. "Why don't you go and get some other quotes. But don't take too long. Eventually the raptors are going to breach one of those chalets and that won't look good in the papers."

Zech and I wouldn't just sit here and let that happen, of course, but...hopefully this director fellow won't dare risk it. Silence from above. Then, "Right, good. Send the contract back signed, then, and we can get started."

A moment later Zech slides down to join us and sits in front of the console, customizing a standard contract with a few quick changes and sending it off to the stingy director fellow. That done, he grabs another sandwich. "Right, I should have time to eat this before that comes back. How's your arm, Isaiah?"

"Fine, Zech. Dressing's not leaking. I should change my pants, though. I got blood on them."

"Okay, do that."

"Then what?" asks Trevor, his eyes darting nervously.

"Then we hunt raptors."

Hunting down twenty raptors through the maze of chalets is every bit as tedious as I expect. At least Father Ben offers to help, so with him driving the 'Vi and me shooting, and Trevor driving his truck with Zech shooting, that gives us the ability to corner them and catch them in crossfire.

As we come near the gates, Father Ben speaks to me on my earpiece. "That 'small' T. rex has finally wandered off." Irony tinges his voice. "Couldn't we just lure a bunch of these raptors outside the same way we did earlier?"

"Yeah, we could, and it would be quicker, but any raptor that's fed on humans is to be culled, says DAPdep. They thought it was their lucky day when they loped through that breach, but it really wasn't. Hah, got you, finally."

I drop what's probably the last Utahraptor, firing twice to make sure of it. The safety rounds we're using shouldn't go through the chalet walls, though I still try not to aim into them, but I don't like them much. They don't kill half so cleanly as a normal HiPiR, or Hide Piercing Round. "I think we're nearly done, anyway. We can evacuate everyone soon, then Zech and I will go house-to-house for one final sweep to make sure nothing's going to wake up hungry in a day or two."

A moment's silence from Father Ben. "You're not going to do that first?"

"Heck, no. That's a recipe for disaster, not knowing if the thing jumping out at you is a raptor or a panicking human. No. By the time we evacuate, any raptors that are left—if any—will be tucked away, sleeping off a big meal, or hiding, wounded. We'll provide cover as people move into the coaches, but it should be very safe. *Then* we check everywhere, top to toe, knowing we can shoot anything that moves, which is the only way to survive a foot patrol."

"Okay, that makes sense. How will you know you've got all the ones that are awake, though?"

"Trust me, today, that's going to be real simple."

Once we're sure we can't find any more raptors, we stop in the middle of the resort and Zech and Trevor rejoin us. It's well past lunchtime, so Zech throws together some more sandwiches while I head up to the turret, peel off the dressing, pry out the clot and get my arm bleeding again. Which all feels just as comfortable as you'd expect, but never mind. It's a really, really good way to make sure no more hungry, wide-awake raptors are lurking.

I eat my sandwich up in the turret, letting the blood smell out through the open windows—not that raptors can't smell an uncovered cut inside a vehicle from about a mile away—then I transfer to the less threatening-looking truck and let Trevor drive me around to every corner of the resort with all the windows open behind the protective grilles, keeping my arm oozing blood.

Nothing rushes—or even peeps—out at us, so I take care of my arm again and it's evacuation time. Before we start, we drop Mei Ling at her parents' chalet—it's past time the kid was reunited with her anxious folks, though she wails at being parted from Dinky. Squirming under her parents' tearful gratitude—"Father Ben went after her first!" I protest yet again—we try to give her the little herbi'saur. We can raise another for the zoo's petting corner, and it'll only grow to the size of a very large, upright dog—but apparently they live in a small apartment and even that is out of the question. Oh dear. Mei Ling wails harder than ever—her parents look anguished.

"Hey, it's okay," I tell the little girl. "Dinky's going to live at Amp-city Zoo; you can visit her whenever you want. We'll tell them all about you when we take her there, so they'll know you're her friend, okay? They might even give you a special pass."

Mei Ling calms down a little, and we make our escape.

Stage one of the evacuation is to make sure the larger central buildings—with their raptor-magnets: kitchens, dining hall, and food storerooms—are empty of people. Okay, if anything got in, it probably went straight to the food, gorged itself silly and lay down to sleep it off, but we still don't want people there until it's been properly cleared.

We quickly locate the night duty receptionist, Susan—the poor woman has spent the morning hiding under the reception desk, clutching her intercom and reassuring people as best she can. She stayed at her post, rather than hiding in the nearest sturdy cupboard, which makes her ten times gutsier than Trevor. She's able to confirm that all the other staff remain in their accommodation—it wasn't quite time for anyone else to come on duty when the breach occurred. The main building hadn't yet been unlocked to the guests, either, so once we've got this lady out, we're done here for now.

Father Ben lets us finish asking our urgent questions, then collars Susan himself, clearly frantic to locate any families who've lost people and do what he can to comfort them. That is his job, I guess. Personally, I'd rather hunt raptors—on foot and with an unreliable rifle.

"Only one family has reported someone...um...missing," Susan tells him.

"Only one? That's good." Father Ben smiles, but I can't let him get his hopes up.

"That probably means in every other chalet it was all or no one."

"Oh." He sighs, then turns to the receptionist again. "Who'd they lose, and where's their chalet?"

"Um, a teenage daughter. She bolted out the back door when the rex came up to the front."

Typical. Even if cityfolk never bothered to read a safety brochure while in-city, you'd think they'd open one before coming to a resort like this and make sure their kids knew what not to do. This sort of tragedy is just so *unnecessary*.

After transferring Susan, clutching a hand-pad with an up-to-date guest list loaded on it, into the 'Vi, we drop Father Ben at the correct chalet on route to the coach drivers' accommodation, covering him until he's inside, then we transfer the drivers to the coach park and see them safely into their vehicles.

With the help of Susan's list, we start loading the right families into the first coach—or at least families who need to go to that city. We certainly don't give a fig who's with which tour company.

After a while, Father Ben turns up the volume on his earpiece mic again. "I think this family should be on the first coach, if possible. They have two smaller children, and they should all get to a proper trauma counselor as soon as possible. But...can you come here and, uh, search the bushes out back? They saw the raptors drag their daughter in there." He drops his voice. "I think they, er, know there's no hope but...well, I don't think they'll leave until it's confirmed. Or if they do, it will just add to their guilt."

Zech sighs. "All right, we're coming."

Giving the coach instructions to follow us, we drive back to the chalet and park behind it so I can cover Zech, who insists on performing the sweep. If there is a sleepy raptor in those bushes, a whiff of blood from my arm will energize it far more than a whiff of sweat from him. Since no heat signatures show on the 'Vi's scanner, he really just doesn't want me to see what there is to be seen, which is dumb because I've seen it all before, but that's a big brother for you.

Zech moves slowly and carefully, peeping inside each ornamental bush. When he reaches the thickest area, he pauses for a moment, then bends to retrieve something from ground-level. Tucking the object in his ammo sash, he finishes the sweep and heads to the chalet. I wish I could turn my earpiece off, but that would be very irresponsible. It's ten times worse for Zech, anyway. He has to tell them—I only have to listen.

"This is Mindy and Jeff." Father Ben introduces the parents. "Mindy, Jeff, this is Zechariah who, as I think you saw, has just conducted a thorough search out back."

"Hi." Zech sounds tense and awkward. "Yeah, uh, I'm sorry to have to tell you, but I found, uh, human remains in the bushes. Do you, uh, recognize this?"

"That's Cindy's shoe," pipes up a child's voice. "Where is she, mister? Mommy and Daddy are worried."

Sobbing. A man's voice whispers, "Yes, that's Cindy's shoe."

"Then I'm afraid it's a positive ID. The coroners will take care of everything here in due course. There's space on the first coach if you want to...to get your kids home."

Two of their kids. More sobbing. But how's Zech supposed to say the right thing, here?

"It's my fault..." It's a woman's voice, all quavery. Oh no, Zech's about to be treated to the whole sorry tale. "When that...that huge *thing* looked in through the window, I shouted: *It's going to break in!* And that's when...that's when she opened the door and ran out... Why did I do it?"

"You thought it was true." Father Ben's voice, very soft. "How could you know any better?"

By cracking open a basic breach security pamphlet,

but hey. Hopefully Zech won't point that out right now.

"I should've gone after her, but I was so busy hanging onto Timmy so he wouldn't run out too... It's my fault..."

"It's not your fault." The man's voice, broken. "It's mine! Once I grabbed Max, right there in the doorway, I saw that raptor running up the path straight towards us and I just...I kicked the door shut. Didn't think about Cindy, just kicked it closed. I could hear it scrabbling at the door, so I ran to the window and two more of them were dragging her into those bushes. And you kept screaming, *help her, go out and help her*! But I just couldn't find *anything* I could fight them off with, and...and I didn't. I didn't help her. I stayed inside."

"Thank God for that," says Zech bluntly. "Or you'd be dead too. Ain't nothing in here you could've fought off one Dakotaraptor with, let alone three. And it would've been too late already."

More sobbing. "He's right." Father Ben's voice is far gentler. "There was no way you could've got your daughter back. You'd only have made your two little boys grow up without a father."

"The very moment she *ran out that door*, it was too late," says Zech. "Nothing you could do. Now, do you want to go on this first coach? Sorry to rush you, but we've got a lot of people to evacuate before dark."

With Zech chivvying them and Father Ben

comforting them, we get them onto the coach. A few more families and it's fully loaded and on its way through the gate. Father Ben goes to help Susan escort each group from chalet door to coach steps as we start on the next one, coaxing along the more nervous individuals and speeding things up no end, though he hands his earpiece over to Susan since we need to confer with her more often, now. Trevor remains in his truck, providing cover from the other direction.

"No one's answering," says Father Ben, some time later. He knocks on the chalet door again.

Susan checks her list. "There should be a family in here."

"Curtains are still drawn. Shall I check round the back?"

"No," I intervene. "Susan, stop him. Stay put, wait for me."

I slide down the ladder before Zech can veto it, and he lets me go, seeing that I'm feeling babied.

"Unlock the door," I tell Susan, once I've joined them, and she does. After she's turned the handle, I wave her back and push the door open with my foot, my rifle ready. At once I see a moving patch of daylight on the lounge floor—the rear door is swinging open. Carefully, I ease forward and look both ways.

"Isaiah, stay outside," Zech scolds me. "Or come back and get the drone."

Blood on the walls. The scent fills my nostrils. Yeah, I've seen enough. I step back and pull the door closed. "Okay, I'm afraid you can put crosses by their names."

"Aren't you going to go in and search properly?" asks Susan. "What if someone managed to hide?"

"The back door's wide open. These flimsy interiors have no door or cupboard strong enough to keep out a raptor longer than a couple of minutes. And there's blood. I'm sorry, there's no need to search. *This* is what that other chalet would look like if the father hadn't kicked that door shut."

Father Ben sighs. "I hope he'll be able to forgive himself one day."

"He saved his wife and both his other kids," I point out. "He shouldn't feel bad."

"I don't think there's any pain like losing a child, Isaiah. Reason doesn't come into it."

I shrug uncomfortably. He's the expert on this. I still think about Mom a lot, I guess. And I feel guilty, 'cause we don't know how she really died, so we're always wondering if there was something we coulda done to stop it. I know I was only eight, but—old enough to have my own rifle, right? I think Zech feels it worse than me, 'cause he was eleven.

Lower lip quivering, her motherly face stricken, Susan marks her list. A whole family. Heck. How many more empty chalets will we find?

One. Only one more. Which I'm inclined to think a minor miracle. *Saint Des, you done good here, today.*

"It was a honeymoon couple," sniffs Susan, as we give the open front door a wide berth. "They were such a *lovely* couple."

Father Ben squeezes her shoulder gently.

The third coach to last is Father Ben's, his diocesan group heading back to Exception State. I watch the young priest shepherding his parishioners to the vehicle and feel like cursing the sun, which is dropping way too fast. There's stuff I'd like to ask him, stuff I'd like to chat about, but we *don't* want to do this in the dark, even with artificial lighting, so with two more coaches still to load, there's not a moment to lose.

That's the last family on board. Susan's already returned to the 'Vi, ready for us to go and fetch the next coach. Father Ben turns and looks up at the 'Vi's turret, where Zech and I hover watchfully. From the way his mouth twists, he's sorry to just part like this, too. But he's got a coachful of tired, frightened people, all desperate to get home to their equally anxious relatives in Exception State, and there's the safety of the last two coach-loads—and the staff—to consider. So, I'm not surprised when he just raises a hand to us in farewell, tracing a quick blessing, and hurries up the steps.

Once the coach door is safely closed, Zech and I wave a goodbye. We follow the coach back to the main drive, where the last two coaches wait, and it heads straight for the gate and disappears into the gathering gloom.

I didn't even get his contact details. But he lives in Exception State and that's a long way away. Guess we're not likely to see each other again. Never mind. More coaches to load.

Soon enough, we're seeing the staff into their minibuses and waving goodbye as they head through the gates into what's getting awfully close to full night. Trevor goes with them. I'm not sure he has permission to skip that final sweep tomorrow or even leave at all, but I guess he's too scared to care. Zech makes no move to stop Mr. Unreliable, nor do I. We're better off without him.

Then it's just Zech and me in the 'Vi, there in a deserted resort. We're used to being alone in the middle of nowhere, but there's something a little creepy about this empty place, with those lightly gnawed human bones lying scattered here and there among the chalets. Not as many victims as we were afraid of, but enough to guarantee that inquiry.

We won't touch the remains ourselves. The moment we can declare the site cleared, the coroner will come and take charge of them. Probably the police will show up, too, to check for foul play. But you don't send extra people into a breach situation until it's been cleared.

Counter-productive, right?

"Okay, final sweep, first light tomorrow," says Zech decisively. "Any critter that's eaten well enough to have already sloped off to take a nap should still be out for the count by then."

Yeah, in an ideal world, we'd have had time to do that sweep tonight, but we're certainly not going out after raptors in the dark, no matter how much illumination the resort boasts.

Ping.

Another message. Something from the resort owners, maybe? But Zech straightens without opening it. "For you."

I go to look.

Did you get my message? I need you to send me $500 asap.

I roll my eyes and hit *delete*. "Spam." I flop down on a chair, wondering if I've got the energy to eat anything. Staying at maximum alert for hours is *exhausting*.

Zech eyes the frying pan unenthusiastically, then pulls lard and cheese from the fridge and puts it beside the small piece of bread left from earlier. "Another sandwich?"

I nod, yawning. "Fine by me."

While he chops the dried-up bread, managing to

extract four wafer-thin slices, I drag myself back to my feet to put instant coffee into two mugs, adding boiling water from the heater tap. I put one in front of Zech as he deposits two slices of bread in front of me.

"So, how'd it go earlier with the priest?" he asks, plonking a chunk of cheese on a slice without attempting to butter it. "He rip strips off you? Was it awful?"

"No." I stare at my bread. "Actually...he wasn't angry with me."

Zech's head turns; he looks startled. "Really?"

"Uh-huh. He obviously thought that I shouldn't have got drunk but that... Uh, he said people always assume it's the guy's fault but sometimes it isn't. He was real mad at Stacey, I thought."

Zech stares at me, frowning. After a moment, he pushes to his feet, balances his sandwich on top of his mug and climbs up into the turret, mug in hand. The hatch clicks as he closes it behind him. My turn to stare after him. But Mister Wilson taught us 'Vi rules, first of which is that if someone wants a private moment, you don't go knocking and whining for them to let you in. It's the only way to live together full-time in such a confined space. So I go back to my sandwich.

Ping.

Another message for me.

Are you getting my messages?

Yes, spammer, I am. I press *delete*. Honestly. Haven't they got anything better to do? I mean, who do they think is actually going to send them money?

I'm too tired to do anything but munch, so I just sit there and munch. I've almost finished a second cup of coffee when Zech climbs back down with an empty mug. He plonks it on the table and drags his chair around, sitting beside me. Then he grabs me and hugs me tight.

"Uh..." Surprised, I return the hug. "Who's dying?"

"Very funny." He lets me go at last and sits back, eyeing me narrowly. "I...just want to say—what the priest said, it made me think. I've been so mad at you for what happened at New Year, giving you a hard time, going on about how disappointed Mom must be. But...if you'd been a girl...and that woman had been a man...it wouldn't be you I'd be mad at, that's for sure. So...I'm sorry, Isaiah."

I swallow a lump in my throat, heat rising in my face. "I did get drunk, Zech. That was wrong. And *stupid*."

"Yeah, it was stupid. But..." He swallows. "I was stupid too, okay?"

Yeah, how *did* Stacey get me out of that bar without Zech noticing? That niggling sense of...of hurt...finally overflows. *"Why didn't you...?"* I bite the words off. He'll think I'm blaming him. No.

But his eyes slide away from mine. He takes a breath. "Yeah, Isaiah, I had a couple too many drinks myself. And one minute you were there just talking to her and then when I looked again, you were gone. I shoulda been your cover, and I let you down big time. I guess that was why I was so angry with you. Easier than being mad at myself. But you shouldn't have paid the price for my stupidity, and I'm really sorry." He takes another deep breath. "No more drinking, okay?"

That old, irrational fear that's tormented me for years stabs me yet again—what if Zech starts drinking? What if he turns into our father? Everyone always said I looked like Mom and Zech like our father, at least in the nose and jaw. So, I just say, "I won't if you won't."

Zech puts his arm around my shoulder again. "Deal."

He stares at me for a moment. "So...uh...are you okay? Uh, y'know?"

"I'm fine, Zech." I still feel that dirty feeling, but not like before. Now God's forgiven me my part in it, it's more like...just the shadow of what I was feeling before. Like I'm just wearing dirty clothes now, instead of having dirt smeared all over my skin.

God and Father Ben forgave me and now Zech has too. I guess I should forgive Stacey, like getting rid of that dirty garment instead of insisting on going around wearing it, and then mebbe I can forget all about it. Yeah. *Okay, Saint Des. I forgive Stacey.*

Oh yeah, and Zech, too. He still looks pretty unhappy. "I'm not mad at you, Zech. You'd never have let it happen on purpose."

"Yeah, sorry, that doesn't make me feel any less responsible, but never mind."

"Mebbe you should go to confession too. It made me feel better."

"I'll think about it, little brother." His tone's gone so unencouraging I guess we're done with this conversation.

Yawning, I stretch, keeping my left arm still so I don't pull the cut open again. "I'm tired; gonna hit the sack. Want me to do the night checks?"

Zech glances at my arm. "I'll do them as soon as I've updated our client. You go to bed."

So I just clean my teeth and my rifle, then shower quickly, slip on fresh clothes and climb up into my bunk. Just in time, I remember my penance and mumble my way through the chaplet of Saint Desmond. My eyelids drag, heavy as lead...

I'm chasing a teenage girl, running as fast as I can, yet somehow she stays ahead of me. "Just stop! Just come back!"

She looks over her shoulder, face twisting in terror. I put a spurt on, trying to catch up, 'cause if I don't, something terrible's going to happen to her, but when I finally get close enough to spring, the arms that bear her to the ground are short and feathered. A huge deadly claw on each toe sinks into her back and my mouth waters as I drop my muzzle towards her warm flesh...

Crack!

Pain stabs me, and I topple over the girl's broken body, my wing-arms fluttering feebly.

"Well, you're a fine specimen and no mistake." A woman, early thirties, slim and heavily made-up, approaches and turns me over with her foot, prodding me with a pink, jeweled rifle tip. "Yes, you'll do nicely."

Stacey grabs my ankle and walks off, dragging me behind her. I screech a helpless protest, but she ignores me, towing me through the dust, bump-bump-bump, until she finally dumps me in a large city-bed. Pink satin smothers me. "There we go. Let's have them, then."

Producing a knife, she lifts one of my three-toed feet and prepares to remove my killing claw. "No!" I yell. "No, don't take them; I'm still alive! Please, don't do it..."

But all that comes from my mouth are raptor-shrieks, and she ignores me.

"Maybe I should put your head on my wall," she muses, ignoring the blood and shoving my precious claws into the pocket of her skinny jeans. The knife moves to my throat and I flinch back...

"You forgot to say yuh prayers, dinna ya?" My father's slurring his words real bad, but I know what he's saying. The sharp bottle edge presses to my neck. My heart hammers in my chest—thud-thud-thud-thud—each beat hurts.

"No, Father," I whisper. "No, I said them. I swear it—"

He clouts me on the ear—I try not to move, but pain spears from my neck as he jolts me against the broken glass. "Lyin's a sin. A sin. Yuh evil. Evil, thru and thru... Ah should cut it outa yuh..."

"No, Father. No, please..."

Is he going to...? Is he really going to...?

The click of a safety catch coming off sounds very loud in the night silence. "Let him go." Zech's voice is cold with fury. I glance his way. The rifle's only a few feet from our father's head. "Let him go or I swear to God I will end this right now!"

Our father glares at Zech, swaying on his feet. "Taking th'Lord's n... Devil's in yuh, boy. Ah should... Ah should..."

"Let him go right now, or you'll be able to tell God how evil I am in person."

Our father's hand twists at my shirt, his eyes glazed with drink and indecision.

"Let him go!"

Our father's other hand clenches on the bottle.

Crack!

Zech fires into the wall beside our father's head.

"LET HIM GO!"

Gasping, I sit up, one hand flying out in time to stop me hitting my head on the roof for the second time in two days. *Yeugh*, what a horrible night's sleep. One nightmare after another. My stomach churns. Memories churn.

Zech and I huddle on the barn roof in a fine drizzle, listening to the drunken man staggering around the farm, shouting Zech's name and shooting at anything that moves or flaps in the wind...

He didn't seem to remember what happened when he woke up—that was normal—but there was something about the way he looked at Zech. Like, deep down he knew his fourteen-year-old son had bested him, and he wasn't going to forget it.

"Pack a bag," Zech told me, that evening. "Pack a bag and keep it ready, but make sure he doesn't find it. First chance we get, we're leaving. If we stay here, someone's going to die."

And less than two weeks later, Zech shook me awake one morning. "Get your bag and your rifle and come with me! There's a HabVi at the gate, come to sell stuff. Father just let it in. We've got to get on board."

Mister Wilson only found us after he'd driven for hours, and the thought of having to drive all the way back made him plenty mad at us. But after Zech made me show him my bruises and scars, and showed his own, Mister Wilson thought better of that. Then he wanted to take us to a city and hand us over to "the appropriate authority" but we begged him to let us work for him instead.

"What if they split us up?" protested Zech. "Anyway, we don't want to go live in a city. They stink. Why not keep us? We're both good shots."

Finally, on the grounds that, "in my book you're a man when you can control yourself and think through the consequences of your actions, never mind what the stupid law says," Mister Wilson agreed to give Zech a trial, with me along as Zech's "dependent." Shortly after that, he paid off his assistant—who didn't want to relocate—and drove from Homa to Rado State, taking us with him. Unless you're a murderer or something really bad, crossing a state boundary guarantees a fresh start, and although we didn't think our father would dare report us missing, Mister Wilson wasn't prepared to risk it. Here in Rado, we went by Zechariah and Isaiah Wilson, and everyone took us for Mister Wilson's nephews of some distant degree.

Although Mister Wilson didn't formally employ me for several years, and I couldn't do everything to start with, any contract I did help with, he paid my due share to Zech with scrupulous fairness, and Zech put the money into a savings account for me. I guess Saint Des was looking out for us, two kids stowing away on a total stranger's 'Vi. I understand enough now to know it coulda gone real bad, but it went real good instead.

Is our father still alive, down there in Homa State? I've not seen him since I was eleven and still he gets into my head. Who cares if he's alive? Just so long as I don't have to go near him again. It's a miracle Zech never shot him.

I shudder and check the time. Six AM. Not many birds singing. Oh, yeah, we're parked in the middle of a resort, that's why. I don't feel like trying to get back to sleep. And we'll need to be starting our sweep about seven-thirty, anyway, soon as it's full light.

Carefully, so I don't thump on Zech's ceiling, I crawl to the bunk door, check the screen—all clear—and climb down quietly, taking my rifle with me.

After flicking the heater on and visiting the head, I open Critter Cage One, releasing Dinky—the cage is an ample size for the baby herbi'saur, but she's a herd animal, so it's better for her to have company, plus the contract is for delivery of a nestling pre-tamed. We've had her for almost two months now, from hatching, and she's a sweetie-pie. After putting some food in her bowl and checking her water trough, I start the coffee machine, sniff the air—yep, fresh bread—and remove the loaf from the food processing unit, belatedly wishing I'd at least put the bread on last night. Zech must've been tired too.

Cutting a thick wedge, I spread it with 'saur lard

and add a smear of jam, then pour a cup of coffee. Butter and marg are both luxuries, as far as we're concerned. Rendered herbi'saur fat makes a decent spread and it's virtually free to obtain. We hunt for our meat and buy grain, milk, eggs, and even fruit from farms. With the food processor we barely need to buy any food in cities. Which saves us a heap of money. All Zech cooks is fried 'saur steaks, anyway, which I know isn't healthy but usually eat all the same.

We saved every cent we could after we started working for Mister Wilson, meaning to buy his 'Vi from him when he retired so we'd have a home of our own. When that day came, five years on, he turned out to have other ideas. "My city-relatives back in Homa have been calling me crazy—and worse names—for years. Don't see why they should have my 'Vi to sell once I'm gone—nor the value of it, either. There's a few more years left in the old girl, and you boys appreciate her. She's yours. Keep your money for when she needs to retire too."

Gobsmacked and appropriately grateful—it turned out he even put off retiring for an extra year until Zech was eighteen—we've spent the last three years saving harder than ever. HabVis are seriously expensive bits of kit, but the newer ones have a lot of extra safety features. Much as we love the old girl, we're looking forward to trading her in. Soon. We've almost got enough. While I'm real sorry people died here, this breach is a big bonus for us.

Munching on my breakfast sandwich, I wake up the console screen with one hand as Dinky nibbles at my pants. Usually, when we're in the middle of nowhere, we have to wait until we acquire a satellite signal to go online, but this resort provides a twenty-four seven connection for its city-guests. I'll check those 'Vi listings again.

I've got two messages, though. I turn at an angle so I can prop my feet on the chair opposite and open the first one. More spam, no doubt.

Are you ignoring me?

Oddly enough, yes. As I delete it and open the next one, Dinky takes a morning run around the living area on her long hind legs, like a rather upright streak of downy beige lightning. Same number again. It's getting annoying.

Why are you ignoring me, Isaiah? I didn't think you were that sort of guy.

I re-read it, rubbing my chin, which is getting bristly again. Huh, that doesn't sound so like a spammer. Or am I being dim? Reluctantly, I type a reply.

Who is this?

I go back to the 'Vi listings, but almost at once the console pings. I check the message.

It's Stacey, don't you recognize my number?

My feet come down on the floor with a thud. *Stacey?* Ugh, so much for not thinking about her again.

No, I threw your number away, I almost send back, but I stop myself. Guess that'll hurt her feelings. Do I care? But I just send back:

Why are you messaging me?

I wait, rubbing Dinky under her beaky little chin until there's another *ping*.

Because you've got to send me $500 asap.

Got to? Seriously? Has she lost her mind? It's not like I *know* her. I barely remember what she looks like. In fact, I wish I'd never met her at all. I try to keep my reply fairly polite, though.

Why on earth would I send you money?

No reply. Maybe she's gone to get dressed or go to work or something. What does she think; that I'm some dumb out-city guy she can fleece? I snort and go back to the listings.

I'm gazing at a shiny 'Vi with a large rear pen and a drone dome on top of its turret housing a proper, long-range drone bristling with cameras and high sensitivity heat sensors—and trying not to drool—when Zech shuffles out of the cab, yawning. He visits the head, just barely avoids tripping over Dinky, then pours himself a coffee, sips—grumbles about it being too weak, of course—and sits at the table, where he cuts a slice of bread and reaches for the cheese. If he's going to forego a fried steak *again*, he really is keen to get a quick start. Less time we give the raptors to sleep off their meals the better. Though with luck there aren't any out there at all.

"We'd better move soon, right?" I say.

Zech nods, eating fast. "We sure had. I'll search, you'll provide cover."

With this cut on my arm, that makes sense, but it means Zech's the one in danger. I note the stubborn set of his jaw and don't waste my breath.

Instead, I fetch Mister Wilson's old short-range drone from the cupboard. Its heat sensors don't penetrate far, but it's useful for something like this, allowing me to check for heat signatures inside any building raptors could've gained access to before Zech enters them. You can't count on the 'Vi's even older heat sensors to go through every wall.

"Okay, we'll do undergrowth and anywhere that's unlocked first," says Zech, swallowing his last bite, "then we can do a full check of all the locked chalets afterwards. Susan left the keycard." He downs the last of his coffee and stands, picking up his rifle.

Yeah, the old open bathroom window scenario. Velociraptors can squeeze through the darndest gaps. Someone goes into a chalet after we've cleared this place and gets half their face bitten off, our reputation will be mud. Zech will check that all the external doors and windows are closed before leaving each building, of course, just to be sure nothing can get in after it's cleared.

Zech pops the clip from his rifle and replaces it with one loaded with normal HiPiRs, then inspects all the mags on his ammo sash, checking they're full of HiPiRs too. I do the same. A foot patrol is no time for messing around with safety rounds.

Before we begin, I take Dinky out and—thinking a silent apology to Mei Ling—I leave her in a piranha'saur-proof pen on the lush, irrigated grass. She can eat her fill—more importantly, if she's still there when we've finished, that's another confirmation that all the raptors are gone, at least the awake ones. "Good luck, girl," I tell her. She blinks unconcernedly and ducks her head to grab a mouthful of grass.

We start the sweep near the gate and move up the hill. Zech alternates between searching and driving the 'Vi on a little way, allowing me to keep eyes on at all times and not have to keep climbing up and down from the turret.

"Okay, clear." I recall the drone and plug the charging cable back into it, then pick up my rifle again as Zech moves through the doorway of a maintenance hut, my eyes darting around as I watch for movement. I've done my best to push Stacey out of my mind. I can't be distracted right now.

Zech gasps—*Crack! Crack!*

"*Zech?*" My heart leaps into my throat, hammering there.

A moment's silence...then Zech blows out a breath. "Okay, false alarm. It was already dead. Crawled in here to die; you didn't miss anything."

I let out my own breath, a heady rush of relief flowing through me. Heck, I hate foot patrols. What hunter doesn't? Most hunters that get killed are killed by raptors—while on a foot patrol. It's crazy-dangerous. But sometimes unavoidable.

I keep my voice steady. "D'you think we can claim

double-bounty on that one since you killed it twice?"

Zech laughs. "Very funny. Okay, this hut's clear, coming out."

We find nothing in the rest of the gardens and other outbuildings, so we turn our attention to the larger buildings in the central complex. I check through the windows with the drone from outside, then I inspect ahead of Zech as much as possible, but there are a lot of closed doors.

"Stop..." I murmur. Zech's in the kitchen storeroom corridor, just on the other side of the wall in front of the 'Vi, and on the drone screen I can make out a smudgy heat signature in the room ahead of him. The door is half-open, so I slip the drone through the gap and the shape sharpens. Long, thin, flat to the ground. Looks like a sleeping raptor to me. Not a little velociraptor either, worse luck. Dakota. I peer at the visual feed, which is on black and white infrared in these dim passages. Where is it? *Hah, there.* I can just spot its head, peeping out from behind a stack of crates.

"Okay, Zech." I speak very softly. "There's a Dakotaraptor asleep in the storeroom ahead of you. When you get to the door, there's a stack of crates along the far wall, then the raptor's head is visible on the floor, sticking out from behind them, about two o'clock. I think you've got a clear shot from the door."

Please, Saint Des, let him have a clear shot. Otherwise

he'll have to choose between going closer or deliberately waking it up and hoping he can get it before it gets him.

Zech doesn't speak, but I see his shadow pass the frosted glass window as he moves silently down the corridor. My heart's in my mouth again. Even worse for Zech, his whole body will be thrumming like a taut wire, flooded with adrenalin. I've been there often enough, though it's amazing how many excuses Zech comes up with to be the one out there on foot.

I pull the drone back to the doorway, not wanting the whisper of its rotors to disturb the raptor, though after a good feed they sleep nice and deeply for several days, usually.

Ping.

I just catch the noise from the console—the speakers are on minimum—but ignore it, my eyes moving between the drone's screen and the building in front of me, checking nothing's sneaking in or out.

The muzzle of Zech's rifle creeps into view on the drone screen. He's taking a moment to make absolutely sure of his aim. I glance at the building again.

Another shadow flits past the frosted window, much bigger—and longer—than Zech's.

My breath stops. Without speaking—if I distract Zech now, he's just as likely to be eaten by the Dakotaraptor—I spin the drone around and raise my rifle, even as my eyes search the screen...a smudge of heat...my eyes pick at the visual...

Yes. *Heck!*

I hope Zech's ready to fire, 'cause that Utahraptor is definitely about to spring.

I aim to the right of the window and put eight rounds through the walls at one foot intervals, coming as close to Zech's approximate position as I dare.

The instant I fire, so does Zech: *Crack-crack!*

The Utahraptor lurches at my last shot...but staggers onwards. Argh, it's too close, I can't fire again, I might hit Zech!

Zech's rifle appears on the drone screen as he spins around, putting two rounds into the looming Utahraptor at horrifyingly close range. It collapses, and he puts a double-tap into its head, then darts into the storeroom to put another shot into the Dakotaraptor there.

"You okay, Zech?" I ask when he finally stands still.

He's breathing hard. "Yeah. Where did that thing come from?"

"Not sure. I saw it passing the window. Stay in there and shut the door while I try and figure it out."

Zech shuts the door without arguing, so he must be rattled.

Chest tight with fear that I missed something — are there any more? — I send the drone along the passage.

There's the kitchen. Zech already cleared that. And the corridor he came down, each storeroom cleared. No, where did the thing come from? Somewhere the thermal imaging couldn't spot it...

Hang on. I move the drone into an alcove, swing it around… Hah. *Not* an alcove. There's a space behind a thick concrete wall to one side. Two big cleaning machines are parked there, and there's a smear of blood between them. We both missed this.

"Okay, Zech, there's a bay with concrete walls at the end of the corridor. It was injured and hiding up in there. Between two big metal machines, just for good measure. That's how the drone missed it. But there aren't any more in there."

Zech sighs. "Right. Let's finish this."

He heads out to check the final wing but finds nothing more. He sweeps this much larger, more complex building again, this time peering into every last tiny velociraptor-sized nook and cranny that could possibly lead to somewhere the heat sensors don't reach—and then it's just a long, tedious check of every locked chalet—doors, windows, and each room.

It's midday by the time we work our way back to where Dinky still grazes placidly, her downy baby-feathers ruffling in the breeze. Zech picks her up with one hand, the pen in the other, and climbs back into the 'Vi.

Setting both the little herbi'saur and her pen on the floor, he drops into a chair, his head flopping back against the nearest unit with a clang. He mutters something under his breath about foot patrolling that probably breaks Mom's fifth rule, but I let it go.

"Call the client on that fancy resort communicator Susan left us," he says after a few moments. "The place is clear."

We've looked absolutely everywhere a raptor could be sleeping, and no awake raptor could've resisted trying to pounce on Zech, the amount he's been wandering around out there this morning, nor Dinky, either. It's clear, all right.

I make the call.

"I saw patching materials in the hut nearest the fence control booth," says Zech, once he's swallowed the last bite of his lunch steak. "Including piranha'saur netting. We should add a strip to the fence."

Piranha'saurs aren't much threat to an adult human unless you panic—or they catch you out in the open—but they're curious little critters, and once the raptor scent disperses, the local shoal will probably show up to check out the patched fence. If a few hop through and nip the cops—or, heaven forbid, the client, if he shows up—it'll be embarrassing.

"I'll do it, Zech." I chase my last piece of steak

down with a final scrap of bread. "You've done your share today."

With the sort of distances we're talking about, out beyond the fence, it's not going to matter if any trace of scent from my cut arm is coming from the turret or the fence, so Zech doesn't argue. It's a quick job, anyway. He covers me while I power down the three sections, clip the netting on along the bottom of the patched area, making sure it doesn't touch the ground, and power the fence back up.

"All done." I kick off the heavy rubber boots and hang the fence security fob back on our key hook.

"Good. We've probably still another hour before anyone gets here, so I'm taking a nap."

He retreats into his cab bedroom, sliding the door shut behind him. Yeah, he turned in even later than I did last night, though I was up earlier. Trouble is, I feel tired but not sleepy. I rub my chin, stubble pricking my fingertips. Huh, at this rate I'll soon have to shave every flipping day. Oh well, it's a sign of manhood, I guess.

I pour myself a coffee and go up into the turret. After opening the windows for fresh air, I prop my feet on the console ledge as I sip and enjoy the view—at least the view in the non-resort direction—enjoying that warm comfortable feeling that comes from completing a dangerous job with everyone alive and still in possession of all their limbs.

When my coffee's gone, I lean my head back and stare up at the turret ceiling, trying to feel sleepy—but it's not happening. With a sigh, I raise my head again. Oh, yeah, a message came in earlier, didn't it? Stacey, again?

Reluctantly, I check the console. Yep, it's for me. *So, Stacey, why do you think I should send you five hundred of my hard-earned bucks, huh?*

I open it.

Because I'm pregnant.

2

BREACH!

"Here, Isaiah. Give me your hand." Mom gently spreads out my fingers and places my palm flat on Jersey's swollen belly, a strand of her long silky hair escaping and tickling my nose. "Do you feel that, sweetie?"

Something moves under my hand. I giggle and press my palm closer, trying to feel it better. "There really is a baby in there!"

"There sure is."

"Zech!" I beckon him with my free hand, then use that to touch the baby as well, transfixed by those little movements. "Zech, come feel! The baby's moving!"

Zech just grins. "Yeah, I've felt calves move before, little bro."

Guess that's true, 'cause he's three whole years older than me and all. I put my cheek against Jersey's side, and the *calf kicks it. "Ow!"*

I laugh, though—so do Zech and Mom.

"The baby's saying hello," Mom says, stroking my hair.

"Yeah?" snorts Zech. "Or 'stop prodding me; I'm trying to sleep in here'."

"When will it be born, Mom? When? How long do we have to wait?"

I open my eyes, coming back from the past. I read the message again. My head spins. My world spins.

Because I'm pregnant.

Stacey's pregnant? There's a *baby? My* baby? Inside Stacey? Right now? My mind's just gummed up. I don't know what to think or do or say. Finally, I reach out and type:

Why are you telling ME?

Okay, I know why, but I have to check. My heart's hammering so hard, my head still spinning. I've no idea when she'll reply. Hardly knowing what I'm doing, I pull out the hand-pad from the shelf under the console ledge and open the book I'm halfway through, then just stare at the page without seeing it. My eyes keep going back to Stacey's message, there on the console. Pregnant. Oh my. What's Zech going to say? He's an uncle. I'm a...a *father*. Cold sweat breaks out all over me.

Ping. I fumble the hand-pad and drop it on the floor as I scramble to check the console.

Because it's you who made me pregnant, stupid.
So just send me the money so I can take care of it.

Five hundred dollars to take care of a baby? Surely it's going to cost way more than that? She must mean five hundred dollars a month. That seems like rather a lot, but...I screw up my face, trying to picture city-life, city expenses.

Food costs a fortune in there. And they have to pay rent. Some apartments don't have enough solar panels to generate all their power, so there's an extra charge for that. Then they all have mobile communicators and all kinds of gadgets, don't they? Clothes. Kids grow out of clothes really fast, right? Childcare when Stacey's working. School stuff...s'pose most of that's later. But...special baby food? And lots of baby...stuff? Maybe she really does need five hundred dollars a month to raise a kid in the city.

I swallow. Oh boy. Zech's not going to like this. It's going to slow how fast I can save, big time. But I can come up with the money, sure. I mean, it's my kid, right? Mebbe we can fit in a few extra contracts. Yeah, we can; no problem.

My mind's still spinning, throwing up a million images, what my kid might look like at all different ages. A girl, a boy? Which is it?

Help me, Saint Des! I didn't expect this. Not for one moment.

Swallowing, trying to keep calm, I type:

Five hundred a month once baby's born if that's what you need but it seems a lot. I don't know city prices so no offense I want you to send some receipts to start with, ok? Do you know if it's a boy or a girl?

I wait, one minute, two minutes, three... Is she still there? Maybe she's typing a longer reply. Maybe she went out. A bleep from the fence fob down below makes me glance over towards the gate. Huh, that was quick. A police jeep and two coroner's vans sit waiting outside. They'd probably already assembled at the nearest fenced settlement to wait for our all clear.

I press the cab intercom button. "Zech, they're here."

Ping.

Okay, I'll just check this, then go help Zech show them around.

Grow up, idiot. I'm not HAVING it! The money is

for an abortion.

Reaching out, I grab at the screen as I read the message. Abortion? To my farm-boy mind, an abortion is something that happens to your cow, making her lose her calf by accident—but, yeah, I know what it means in the city. In the city—it's deliberate.

My fingers hook into claws, scratching at the words, and I bend over, my stomach churning.

An *abortion*? She wants to have an *abortion*? To kill her baby, our baby, my baby?

No, no, no, no...!

Saint Des, help! Why, why would she do that?

*Hang on...hang on...*I grip the console ledge, trying to calm down. It's obvious, right? She can't afford it. She can't even afford the... Yeah, that's why she's asking me for the money. I'll have to pay for everything, that's all.

"Isaiah, aren't you coming down?"

I swallow. Try to keep my voice steady. "Uh, I've just got to take care of something. I'll be right behind you."

"Take care of what?"

Zech's footsteps approach the turret ladder. Panicking, I grab the hatch and swing it down, turn the handle. Click. *Sorry, bro. I've gotta...I've just gotta sort this.*

"Isaiah? You okay?"

"Fine, Zech. Go deal with that lot, will you?"

I hear Zech's frustrated sigh even through the heavy hatch. But when I glance out of the window, the outer gate's opening and the first couple of vehicles are driving in. Zech can show them where to go.

Leaning over the screen again, I type:

It's okay Stacey, you don't need to do that. I can
pay all your medical bills and everything. And the
kid's expenses when it's born. Just send me all
the bills and receipts and stuff.

I sit back, my insides unknotting slightly. Guess she's more strapped than I realized. All those city apartments look fancy to me.

Ping.

Are you crazy, Isaiah? I'm not having a baby right
now!

I scowl at the screen, my stomach clenching in dread. I type back:

Yeah? Seems like you are.

Ping.

No, cos I'm having an abortion, stupid. Just send

me the $500 and forget it.

Forget it? How could I forget something like that?
My hands shaking, I type:

You are not getting one single cent of my money
to kill our baby. I will pay all your medical
expenses for you to have it and if you don't want
it, fine, give it to me when it's born. I'll take care
of it.

I whack *send*—then stare at the message on the
screen, my stomach in free fall. What am I saying? A
baby? *Me*, with a baby? Can I raise a baby?

The shakes spread from my hands to my whole
body.

A baby? I'm eighteen! I live in a HabVi!

But...an abortion?

I feel like an ant being ground between two stones.

No. I can't let her do that. I can raise a baby if I have
to, right? I mean, people have been doing it since year
one. How hard can it be? I mean, Zech practically raised
me. Once I was older...

Ping.

I'm having an abortion, Isaiah, with or without
your money. Seven more months pregnant? No

thanks. It's your fault, so pay up.

My fault? Anger explodes inside me. I kick the turret wall and promptly regret it. Ouch. *My* fault?

But I read the message again and the anger gives way to fear. She *doesn't* need my money to do it. That's what she's saying. She just wants me to pay for it anyway.

Panicking, I start typing again:

All your medical expenses, and a living allowance or whatever, for the seven months so you don't have to worry about work. Or for a full nine months, okay? We can sign something to say I'm taking the baby and you won't have to have anything to do with it ever again. That's fair, isn't it?

Send.

That's fair, surely? I know it's her who has to be pregnant, not me, but if I even pay, like, her salary while she's *being* pregnant... That's fair, right?

No reply. My stomach fluttering uncomfortably, I watch Zech hop into the police car, pointing up the main drive as he directs them to the closest site of a fatality. His head turns as though he's staring at the turret, but he's too far away to see my face. He raises a hand and taps his ear.

Ugh, he's right, my earpiece is off. Reluctantly, since he is out-vehicle now, I switch it on. Will he ask me what's going on? Big brothers, y'know, don't always stick to 'Vi rules. But he's busy directing the cops and answering their questions. He's turned his earpiece's mic right down, anyway, so I don't have to listen to it all, and I do the same, afraid I might start yelling at the console or something.

I stare at the screen. *Come on, Stacey, say yes. Don't kill our baby, please.* My baby. Yeah, if she doesn't want it, it's *my* baby, really.

My mind's still spinning. I've barely thought about kids, except vaguely, years in the future, I assumed I'd have some. I have this little fantasy that Zech and I will meet a pair of lady hunters, and we'll marry them and get a second 'Vi and hunt together. 'Course, the truth is virtually no women actually take up this way of life, those that do aren't the kind to have much time for Mom's rules, and every other hunter is vying for their affections, anyway. No chance.

More realistically, I've always hoped either Zech or I will one day find a nice farm girl to marry. Then the kids can grow up on the farm, just going on hunting trips now and then. Some hunters keep families in the city, it's true, but I wouldn't want that.

But I *have* a kid now, so I've gotta deal. Kinda like

getting out of the 'Vi when unSPARKed—the moment you step out, you're committed.

Stacey, say yes...

Bleep. The faint sound comes from below. That's the fence fob again; Zech left it here. I glance towards the gate. Yes, a fence maintenance vehicle and a sleeping van wait outside. Swallowing, I open the hatch and slide down to retrieve the fob. Looking out through the little window by the rear door, I open the gates for them, outer and then inner, my heart sinking when they drive straight over to the 'Vi.

A voice comes over the Intercar. "Hello, the HabVi? Anyone at home? Can we start work?"

Opening the side door, I go out to meet them. They need the fob, anyway.

"Start work as soon as you like," I tell them. "My brother's showing the police and coroners around, but I can cover you just fine."

They smile and nod—I offer them coffee, but they've got their own facilities in the van. So I head back up to the turret with my rifle and set the movement sensors.

Still no reply from Stacey.

"We okay to power down sections thirty-six to thirty-eight?" The techies are out by the fence now, all bright yellow boots and heavy tool belts.

"Whenever you like. You're covered."

"Powering down now."

That means other than a few feeble wires, I'm all that stands between them and any hungry carni'saur that wanders along. I struggle to push Stacey out of my mind and keep my eyes on the valley, to keep watching the distant hillside, to keep checking each boulder and tree and stand of tall winter-browned grass.

Stacey, I can put out of my mind. Not my baby. That tiny, helpless scrap of flesh and blood, miles away in Amp-city, nestled inside Stacey.

Saint Des, please? Please, please, please...

I can teach my little boy or girl to be self-sufficient, to shoot, to perform live captures, to appreciate all the wonderful creatures we share the countryside with. To sit in the turret in the darkness and see every star in the sky. To swim in a clear, fresh stream. To read, to write—we can read stories together!

Concentrate, Isaiah. I scan the valley all over again. Movement sensors are all very well, but I have to pay attention.

What's that? Herbi'saurs. A herd of wild iguanodons, smaller and rangier than the ones we used to raise when I was a kid. Great. They're going to amble right up and...

The movement alarm begins to emit frequent squawks. Yep, nothing for it. I need to get rid of them.

I press the Intercar button. "Attention, everyone in

Green Acres Resort, I'm going to fire at a herd of herbi'saurs. There is no cause for alarm."

"We hear you, Isaiah," says Zech, in my ear. The techies just turn and give me a thumbs up. They can see the problem.

I raise my rifle, checking the muzzle is through the bars. Plenty of meat on one of those things. I could drop a small one. But I'm not too sure when Zech or I will be free to go out and bring it in, let alone have time to butcher it, and the winter sun is warm. It might spoil— or attract carni'saurs. Nah, I'll just chase them off.

Locating what looks like the lead female, I aim for the ground near her feet.

Crack!

No need for a second shot, she's up on her hind legs and running, the herd streaming behind her.

Sorry, ladies. I know there's a lot of grass there. You can come back another day, huh?

What will the child look like? Stacey's quite a bit lighter than me. Will it have her eyes? Mom's eyes? My nose? Zech's jaw?

Ping.

Argh, I bet that's Stacey. I can't look now, not while I'm covering these guys. I can't.

I fight to keep my eyes on the grassy valley slopes. My foot jiggles up and down; I can't stop it. The message, the console, just there on the ledge, itches at my mind. Heck, surely not reading the message is a worse distraction than reading it?

Or maybe that's just the devil whispering to me.

I keep my eyes out-fence — until I realize I'm barely seeing what I'm looking at.

Saint Des, help!

Desperately, I swipe the console, letting the message pop open. I scan the view outside again and only then allow myself to snatch a glance.

No.

One word, that's all. My heart clenches, my gut clenches, everything clenches. No? *No?* She'd rather kill our baby than have an all-expenses-paid nine-month — okay, hardly vacation, but still? Or pocket a nice bonus if she kept working throughout? *No?*

I drag my attention back to my task, but my distraction's even worse now. I can barely take in what I'm looking at.

Father Ben's voice plays in my mind: *I don't think there's any pain like losing a child.*

Am I about to find out? *O God, please?* Yes, this is too serious just for Saint Des. *God? Please?* I want to type a reply, say something to change her mind, but I can't. Not while I'm providing cover. I've *got* to keep my eyes peeled.

My baby. My baby my baby my baby my baby…
I can't, I just…*can't*…

I drop my hand to the keypad. One letter—a careful look around—another letter—another check. Slowly, my reply appears on the screen.

Stacey, you don't want our baby, but I do. Please don't kill it. I will pay for EVERYTHING. As many months after as you need to recover, too. I will take the baby away and we will never bother you about anything, ever. Just let our child live, please?

Send. My blood thunders in my head as I wait, forcing my brain to process the visual information it's receiving from my eyes by sheer effort of will. Nothing's moving out there, thank God.

Stacey, please, please, please, it's your baby too…
Squawk.

Huh? My eyes fly over the landscape, but I see nothing. Hmm. That tree branch is moving. The wind's getting up. I've gotta, gotta, gotta concentrate. The wind will soon make the movement sensor useless.

God, please?
Ping.

I swipe at the screen, somehow manage to give everything another once-over, then I look.

It's just a clump of cells, Isaiah! I'm not barfing and getting fat and getting stretch marks and waddling and not drinking for seven months, forget it! I've made the appointment for Thursday. If you don't take responsibility and cough up the money you're total scum.

Tears blur my vision as I check for danger again. The movement sensor squawks. I swipe a hand over my eyes and try to focus. I can't see anything; it's probably just the branches moving. Another squawk. Yeah, the thing's useless now. I need to do this manually, as it were, but...

I sniff, fighting to get hold of myself, but it's no use. What can I do? What can I *do*?

Nothing. Absolutely nothing. I can't stop her going to that place in two days and killing my son or daughter. When it comes to this, what I think doesn't matter. I have no rights at all. I'm the father, I'm nobody.

Isaiah! You're supposed to be covering these guys!

I struggle to see through my tears, but I can't stop them. I feel utterly helpless, as though I'm staked out, alone, in the middle of nowhere, smeared with fresh blood and with twenty packs of raptors closing in around me.

I can't save my child. My baby will die on Thursday and there's nothing I can do.

I need to get the techies to come back in. This isn't safe. But when I dash the water from my eyes and peer down at the fence, they've removed almost all the temporary wires already but put nothing in their place yet. There's nothing there for them to switch on—I'm all that's standing between not just the carni'saurs and *them*, but all those cops and coroners and Zech as well.

Heck! I don't like it, but I know what I have to do. I put a hand to my earpiece and raise the mic volume.

"Zech?" I try to speak calmly but my voice wobbles and cracks, the salty taste of tears filling my mouth. "Can you come back here?"

"*Isaiah?* What's wrong? *Are you hurt?*"

"No, m'fine, I jus'...jus' need you to come and cover this big hole in the fence. I can't..." I sniff, trying to clear my throat. "I can't concentrate. S'not safe, Zech. Come back, quick."

"I'm on my way. Are you sick?"

"No. Jus' come." I stare out, wiping my eyes over and over, trying to see what I need to see.

Soon one of the naked resort trucks pulls up by the 'Vi, and Zech jumps out. And then he's climbing into the turret, his anxious gaze dissecting my face.

"Isaiah...?"

"Jus' cover the breach," I whisper. I slide down the

ladder, climb up into my bedroom, shut the door, turn off my earpiece mic and lie with my face in my pillow so Zech won't hear me crying.

I always thought I'd be a better father than my own—one day. That I'd love my kids, take care of them—but I'm going to fail right now, right at the very beginning. I'm helpless—I'm useless. *I got drunk, me,* and my kid's going to pay for it.

I pound my fist into my pillow, my mattress, but it doesn't *help*—into the metal walls—*clang, ouch*—again and again. *Clang. Clang. Clang...*

"Isaiah?" Zech's voice in my ear.

I pull out my earpiece and shove it under the pillow, but I stop hitting the walls. There's blood on my knuckles already. I ram my face back into the bedding and cry some more. I haven't felt like this since Mom died. At least Mom will look after my baby.

But I don't want Mom to look after my baby. *I* want to look after my baby!

Mom, please pray for us!

The only reason I don't ask Mom for prayers more often is because it hurts too much to think about her. But I can't hurt any more, right now, so:

Mom, pray, please?

The creak of the turret ladder and a knock on my bedroom door drag me from a fog of misery. How much time has passed? Hours?

"Isaiah?"

I pull my sleeping bag over my head. Zech can't help me. Not this time.

I hear the door slide back; feel him perch in the entrance of my berth. The light clicks on, seeping in on me.

"The coroners have finished up and taken themselves off, along with what's left of those poor folks. Cops are still taking pictures. Fence guys have got all the major wires up and clipped some temporary netting over it—they say it's a good point at which to stop for the night. Mebbe, or mebbe they just figured out there's a pool in the central complex, but if they say so. Fence is back up, anyway. So, we're off-duty until tomorrow, now."

A twinge of guilt stirs—I've left Zech up there for hours, without any break to use the head or snack or just relax for a moment. I guess he just peed out the window, but still. If I open my mouth, I'm afraid I'll start crying again, and I'm not a cry baby, so...so I keep it shut.

Silence for a while. Then he gives my leg a squeeze. "Isaiah? I...read the messages."

Yeah, well, I left them up on the screen, so that's no surprise. Figured he had or he'd'd've been in here by now, checking I wasn't dying or something.

"I'm really sorry, cub. That woman's a piece of work, all right. I'd like to punch her lights out, only I guess that would break rule three."

I still can't speak.

Zech sighs. "Look, you tried. Some folks just can't be reasoned with and that's a fact." He hesitates. "And...maybe it's for the best. I mean, what we going to do with a baby, huh?"

I sit up and kick him clean out of my berth. "That's my *child*, Zech!" I yell after him. "Your niece or nephew's got a death sentence and that's *for the best?* You sound like *her!*" I scramble along and try to pull the door shut, but he pops up again before I can.

"Yeah, okay, sorry, Isaiah." His face blazes hotly. "That wasn't a nice thing to say. Of course it's bad. It's really bad. I'm sorry. But you did everything you could, okay?" He reaches for my battered hand, trying to get a better look, but I yank it away. He draws back again. "Okay, look, why don't you come check out that pool; take your mind off it for a bit?"

"No."

"Do you mind if I go?"

"Yes, fine, *go*. Have fun. Bye." I push him out of the way of the door and slide it shut.

"Isaiah..."

"Just go away. I'm fine."

Zech sighs and clatters around in the living area for

a while. Eventually, he taps on the door again. "Okay, I'm heading over to the pool; sure you don't want to come?"

I ignore him.

"I left you a coffee on the table. I'll see you in a bit."

I hear the 'Vi door hiss open—then closed. I'm alone.

Flopping down on my back, I stare up at the metal ceiling lining. Behind it is a layer of sound and heat insulation, then the protective outer metal skin that's proof against small to medium-sized 'saurs.

Surely only the worst dads aren't able to keep their kids alive long enough to even be born?

Really? Even though I've no rights and no say?

I still can't help *feeling* that way, though. Guess Father Ben was right. Reason doesn't come into this. No, that's not quite true, is it? I mean, claiming you can kill someone because they're very young, *that's* irrational, right?

Some folks just can't be reasoned with. That's what Zech said. *You've done everything you can.*

Have I? Have I really?

Stacey's last message plays in my mind and my heart sinks. Zech's right. She's not going to be reasoned with. So, what else can I do? Nothing, right?

Something niggles at my mind, though. *Some folks can't be reasoned with.* That's pretty much a saying, I guess? There's another saying, hovering just out of reach. A bit similar, mebbe? What is it?

It won't come. I thump my mattress in frustration. *Ow.*

Coffee. Zech mentioned coffee. Maybe it will, like, jog it loose in my head. I slide back the door and jump down. My mug's there on the table, full, and beside it stands a box of ScentBlock Band-Aids and a bowl of my favorite apple, raisin n'cream dessert, that Zech's whipped up in the processor. The sight loosens the ball of anger in my chest, but I don't feel hungry.

I grab the mug and sip without sitting down. *Come on, what...*

Everyone has a price.

Yeah, that's the saying. No, I haven't done everything, tried everything, have I? Okay, I'd rather Stacey spared our baby because it's the right thing to do. But at this point, who cares *why*, just so long as she *does.*

So...what's Stacey's price?

I put the mug down and sit at the console, waking up the screen. I read her last message again.

It's just a clump of cells, Isaiah! I'm not barfing and getting fat and getting stretch marks and waddling and not drinking for seven months, forget it! I've made the appointment for

Thursday. If you don't take responsibility and cough up the money you're total scum.

Not low. Her price is not low. I'm sure of that much. I already gave a generous offer. If she was going to accept anything reasonable, she'd've gone for it already.

I need to really, really up the stakes. I open my savings account and check the figure, though I know it by heart.

$40,060.56

That's almost half our new 'Vi, sitting in there. A bit less than half. Since I couldn't help with as many contracts as Zech to start with, he's got more saved than me. Still. Seven years, I've been saving this money. But I've been able to earn much faster since I got older, and now we're only splitting the money two ways—instead of half to Mister Wilson, as the owner of the 'Vi, and only a quarter each to Zech and me—that helps a lot.

I read her message yet again. If I offer too little, she's just going to say no. Oh, Zech's not going to like this.

Saint Desmond, let me get it right.

I take a deep breath, and type, ignoring my painful knuckles.

Stacey, I will pay the medical expenses and give you $20,000 if you have the baby for me.

I stare at what I've written. Twenty thousand dollars. Half my savings. Should I try ten thousand dollars first? I read her message again. No, my gut says ten thousand dollars isn't enough. It seems crazy—I mean, who'd refuse ten thousand dollars to *not* kill their own child?—but I trust my instincts. It's gotta be more.

Should I do this? Should I press *send?* Am *I* crazy to even consider it?

I don't think there's any pain like losing a child. Reason doesn't come into it.

Oh boy, you said it, Father Ben. One thought of the pain and anguish and helpless hopelessness I've drowned in all afternoon, and my hand stabs the button.

Ping, away it goes.

I stare at the screen, trying to breathe, terrified by what I've just done. Twenty *thousand* dollars?

No, I don't care. It's only money, right? I can earn more. But I can't replace my child. That's not how it works.

How long would it take Stacey to earn twenty thousand dollars? I'm sure she said something about working in a top-notch restaurant as a...she used a fancy name but it sounded like a waitress to me. Hunters aren't really as well off as everyone thinks, when you factor in the costs of buying and running a HabVi, but it's hardly a low-paid job. With her city-lifestyle, I'm guessing it would take her at least as long as it took me to earn that money. Mebbe a lot longer. If she can earn it in seven short months, she's not likely to say no. Right?

Please, God. Let that be true. I sit and stare at the screen, my stomach churning.

Maybe she's busy.

Maybe she needs to think about it.

She might not reply for hours.

I should try to eat that dessert or Zech will think I haven't forgiven him. Though I guess it's him that needs to forgive me, now.

Slowly, still staring at the screen, I fumble for the bowl. Half the first spoonful smears over my cheek. I'm going to have to look at what I'm doing.

When I manage to swallow a mouthful, I realize how hungry I am. I dig the spoon in again. And again. And again. The food actually has a settling effect on my stomach. When it's gone, I wash up the bowl and finish the coffee, then clean my cuts and apply Band-Aids. Artificial skin doesn't work well on fingers, tends to fall off. Taking an odor neutralizing wipe up into the bedroom, I go over any bit of wall I might've bled on, then change my sleeping bag cover and pillow case, bundling the maybe-bloodied ones into the washer.

Once that's all done, I try to read but can't concentrate, so I get Dinky out of her cage and let her sit on my lap while I stare at the screen, waiting. She'll get lonely if she's left in there too long. I'd let her run around, but she might slip out when Zech comes back in.

When I resist her initial attempts to get down and explore, she folds her long hind legs comfortably under her and chills out happily enough, with her head in the crook of my arm, her warm herbi'saur scent pleasant in my nostrils. I rub her head and try to picture my tiny child. It's been a long time since Zech made me swipe through a biology textbook, but I guess it's probably still at the age where it's all curled forward and bald, with translucent skin, like a tiny stooped old person curled up in there, but without the big ears.

Mebbe Stacey's never seen a miscarried calf or opened an egg that failed to hatch. Mebbe she really believes it's just some little clot. Is human biology mandatory in city schools? I guess not.

What's Zech going to say?

Uh-oh. The side door slides back. Here he is.

A flash of relief crosses his face when he sees me sitting there. He wedges his towel roll on the turret ladder, to deal with later, and comes straight over to me. "You've come back to life, then?"

I nod. Suddenly I'm regretting the dessert, after all, but... "Uh...thanks for the apple mush."

Zech shrugs. "The cops have gone, now." He eyes

me closely, then his eyes dart to the screen—he bends to read the last message.

I hold my breath, fighting an urge to close my eyes too.

His lips mouth the figure. Finally, he swings round to look at me again.

"*Isaiah!*" It's almost a moan.

"I had to."

"You didn't have to! Not that! That's over and beyond, that is!"

"No, it's not. You said I'd done everything I could. But it wasn't true."

"And what about our new 'Vi, little bro?"

"If we take every contract we can, work really hard, we'll be able to get it in only a few, um...years...more."

Zech stands there and shuts his eyes. He wants to yell and scream, I can tell. We've worked for that new 'Vi, sweated for it, bled for it, for *years*. Now I'm driving a tank through all that, for a little person who's hardly real to him yet. Can't blame him for that; the baby's barely real to me, however tightly it's grabbed my heart in its still-forming hands.

Zech breathes deeply, his face screwed up. He's trying to be understanding, trying not to be angry. Trying to be a good brother. He bites his lip and finally opens his eyes again. Glares around at the shabby metal interior. "Then I guess we'd better get used to the idea of a baby in here. 'Cause there's no way she's going to turn *that* offer down."

He grabs his towel roll and for a moment I'm sure he's going to chuck it my way, but his eyes dart to Dinky, and he simply stamps into the cab and locks the door behind him.

I guess...that could have gone worse.

I squint guiltily at the little window. I've done nothing all afternoon. There's an hour's daylight left. I can go out and deal with some dead raptors, surely?

Oh joy.

The she-raptor grabs for the baby in my arms. I pull back and sprint away, but she appears in front of me, seizing the baby in her mouth.

"No!" I try to grab it back, but she giggles and dashes off.

I run after her, run and run as fast as I can. "Give it back!"

Darting up a spire of rock, she looks down at me. "You're pathetic! You could've saved your baby if you had claws! But look at you!"

I look. My leathery, three-toed feet have only two short claws and an empty toe. Where are my killing claws? My pride and joy?

"What use are you?" crows the she-raptor. "What use are you to anyone, a male without claws? You'll never get a mate now!"

I struggle to climb the spire of rock, unable to balance properly without my huge claws. Finally, I'm at the top. But as I reach out with my wing-arms to take the baby from her, it disappears like mist touched by the sun.

"No!"

I jerk awake, shivering and clammy. Ugh. Sitting up, I scramble quickly to the door. Stacey hadn't replied when I finally went to bed. Maybe she's replied now.

Dropping down quietly, I wake up the console. It's six AM. Huh, no reply.

Is that good? She's thinking about it?

Or bad? That she *needs* to think about it?

Zech thought she'd grab the offer. I kinda thought so too.

The fence guys won't start work before eight, but there's no way I can go back to sleep. I open Dinky's cage door and feed her, then make a coffee and a sandwich and climb up to the turret. I put the hand-pad in my lap but end up staring out the window, my thoughts cycling through worry-prayer-worry-prayer-worry as the sun creeps up towards the horizon, casting spectacular pale orange-gold-yellow pre-dawn patterns over everything.

Ping.

The mug slips from my hand—I manage to grab it...*phew*...just. Plonking it on the console ledge, I swipe quickly at the screen. It's from her!

Isaiah, I really wonder about your sanity. But I have to say no. Sorry. Weight gain? Stretch marks? I told you I'm a model, right? Think it through, baby boy.

I choke, my throat constricting as I stare at her message. *No? She's saying no?* I could swear she said she worked as a waitress. A model? I guess she must do that too. I've some vague memory, now I think about it, of her showing me pictures, while I tried to force down some breakfast to be polite, hoping she'd let me go home once I had. I'd a pounding headache and felt sick as a dog and so upset about it all—but I remember trying not to really look at the shots she seemed so proud of, 'cause in some of them she had clothes on, but in some she, um, didn't. Not many, anyway.

Is she saying her career's at stake? Surely models have kids, don't they? But if she's convinced she can't, if she values her career more even than *twenty thousand dollars*? Then there's no hope, no hope at all...

That black cloud of pain and despair rears over me like a striking snake, preparing to engulf me once more.

Mom, Saint Des, God, please?

God lost his son, didn't he? He must understand...

I never gave up on you. The words whisper through my mind, not quite fitting with my own thoughts.

Giving up? Is that what I'm doing? But what else can I do?

Everyone has their price.

My skin prickles coldly, every hair standing on end. Oh yeah. That. Guess we're not done yet. Or are we? How can I do this to Zech? Disappoint him like this? Make him work so much harder and longer for our dream? We can't even keep this old girl going for more than another decade, absolute tops.

It wouldn't take a decade to earn it back. Not these days. And what if it did? Are you putting a price on your baby's life? Shouldn't you leave that to Stacey?

Money. Only money…

…I'm crying, my face smooched against Mom's chest. "But I was going to buy a piranha'saur of my very own, Mom! I've been saving for months *and* months*! And now I can't. And I* did *genuflect! I did, Mom! Don't you believe me?"*

"Shhhh, sweetie. I know you did. Daddy's not well right now; we all have to be patient with him. You know he's going to a special hospital very soon. When he comes back, he'll be better."

"But he took all my savings! All of it! Con…confis…cted it!"

"Money is only money, Isaiah. Don't ever cling to it, or it'll break your heart, hmm? When Daddy's better he'll buy you a piranha'saur, you wait and see."

Only Mom died—somehow—and he never got to that rehab centre, did he? I stare at my hands, knotted in my lap, cold from the memory. Mom was the bright, warm centre of our family, of my life. Losing her was like... I'd have paid any amount to save her, given up this 'Vi, anything. How will I feel on Thursday evening, with my forty thousand dollars in the bank and my child dead?

I lean over the screen and type:

I will pay you $40,000 and your expenses. Don't think if you say no I'll offer more. I can't offer more, that's all my savings. I'm not lying. We can split it in three, soon as we have the paperwork signed you get the first third, then part of the second third each month, then the last third when the baby's born. Please say yes.

I attach a photograph of my savings account balance, with the account numbers grayed out.

And I press *send*.

Zech is going to *kill* me.

By seven she still hasn't replied. I might as well have gone out and got on with something. Oh well. Dinky's been cooing plaintively at the bottom of the ladder for a while, so I finally fetch her up.

"Sit still, little one," I murmur, settling into the chair again with her on my lap. "Or you'll fall right down that hole in the floor, hmm?"

Zech shuffles out at about seven-thirty. "What did she say, then?" he calls through the hatch.

"I'm still, uh, waiting for her final answer." Okay, so maybe it's cowardly to put off telling him what I've done, but if she says no—*God, don't let her say no!*—there's no point stressing him out, is there? "I can do the first stint if you want to sleep-in," I add.

Zech yawns and stretches. "I might head to the pool again, actually. Nice to swim without worrying what's sneaking up on you."

"Okay, now I'm really offended." I put on a hurt tone. "Since when have I ever let anything sneak up on you while you were in the water?"

Zech just grins and flaps a hand at me.

At eight, the fence guys emerge from their van ready to work. I shut Dinky back into her cage and take my rifle up to the turret. The wind's died down this morning, so I can set the movement sensors again.

"Okay to shut down sections thirty-six to thirty-eight?" asks the head fence guy on the Intercar. "How are you today, by the way? Your brother said you weren't well?"

"I'm much better, thanks. And yes, you're good to shut it down."

Nothing happens for two hours. Stacey doesn't reply and virtually nothing moves beyond the fence. Guess we wiped out all three of the local raptor packs the other day and it'll take time for their territory to be filled, though not that much time.

At ten o'clock, a mature male allosaur lumbers across the far side of the valley—twenty-six feet long with four-inch teeth—but it only looks towards the fence once and doesn't stop. There're always humans over here, but the fence is always on, so why would it think today would be any different? Neither curious, nor that bright, allosaurs.

Zech climbs up soon, so I take a break, but before long I rejoin him. I don't have the heart for sporting around in the pool, right now. I could go and deal with some more raptor carcasses, but I can't drag myself away from the console for that either. The turret's the place to be on a nice day, anyway, and two pairs of eyes never hurt.

The fence is coming on well. They've fitted several feet of the finer cross-wires already. They always work top down for the small wires, since a rex is more likely to turn back if it sees the fence and the more wires you get in place high up the more likely it will notice it. Which is a good theory, but...

Raising my rifle, I look through the telescopic sight, focusing on... Hard to make out at that distance, but...twelve inches tall, mostly thin legs and neck, standing upright on its rear legs, it looks superficially like a baby leggy'saur, like Dinky, only without feathers. But it's not. And there's never just one piranha'saur.

I press the Intercar button, my voice booming from their van's speakers. "Fence team, please power up the fence if you can and get inside your vehicles. There's a shoal of piranha'saurs incoming."

Zech turns his sights in the same direction. "Oh yeah. Three of the critters."

By the time I look again, it'll be five. Then ten. Then fifty...

Sighing, the fence team switch the fence back on and retreat to their van. It's not long before the shoal flows down the hillside, a swarm of black specks that turn into little upright carni'saurs as they get closer. They run along the fence, getting very close, cocking their tiny heads and peering at it. No question they could jump through, if they really wanted. Let's hope none of the repair guys have dropped a sandwich.

"Look at them thinking about it," says Zech, shaking his head. "Sure, you little vermin, come on in, the more the merrier."

Yeah, if any do hop through, we can just catch them and sell them to a pet store. Single piranha'saurs make great pets for boys.

Evidently none of the repair guys are dim enough to take food near the breach they're repairing. At any rate, the piranha'saurs flow away up the valley and are soon out of sight. Zech gives the all clear and the guys go back to work. By lunch time, the little wires on the fence are over half completed. As most of them head for their van and Zech drops below to make a start on lunch, I stay up in the turret, waiting for the head guy to power up the fence.

"Fence back up."

"Good. We'll provide cover again in an hour."

With a wave to the turret, the guy heads to join his co-workers.

Ping.

My heart leaps into my mouth, thumping there like a dying fish. *O God, oh Saint Des, oh Mom...*

It's for me. It's from Stacey.

I open it.

You're insane. I hate you. $40,060.56 plus expenses and I'll have the thing but I never want to see it again. Get the paperwork sorted out. I want the first payment asap, before you come to your senses.

I sink back into the chair, shaking, shuddering, waves of relief and terror colliding inside me. She even wants the sixty dollars and fifty-six cents? That is just petty. But I'm not quibbling over it. I reach out and type:

> $40,060.56 plus expenses, agreed. I'll head in-city tomorrow and sort everything out.

Send. I've done it. I've saved my baby. Now...now I've just got to...be a good father.

And—carefully, I close the message thread—tell Zech.

"So?" asks Zech, busy dumping lard into the frying pan when I slide down the ladder. "Was it her, finally? What did she say?"

I swallow. My mind's going round and round, every part of me churning. Father—me! Baby—safe! Baby—*here*... I can't have this conversation now. So I simply say, "She accepted my offer. I need to go in-city and see a lawyer."

"Right." Zech nods. Blows out a breath. "Right. Okay. So. Baby incoming. I'm trying to be happy for you, bro, really. Huh, this is crazy. Have you thought about adoption?"

"No. That's fine if you *can't*. We can."

"In a HabVi? Two guys?"

"Back up our family tree are people who raised

babies in *tepees*. Always on the move, season to season. And people from Africa, who were surrounded by predators. Even our European ancestors were nomadic *once*. Ask them if we can raise a baby in a HabVi with modern weapons, electric light, and full mod cons and they'd laugh in your face."

Zech sighs. "You want a steak, right?"

I almost say yes, but I stop myself. "Eggs. I'll have eggs. And I'm gonna boil them."

Zech wrinkles up his nose. "Okay, why?"

"'Cause I wanna live long enough to see my kid grow up, is why."

Zech gives the world's biggest ever eye roll. "Suit yourself, little brother."

"Right, we'd better get down to it," says Zech, as we wash up. "Since I assume you're mad to get to Amp-city tomorrow?"

"Yeah, I am. I'll go get started on some more of those raptors."

Zech's silent for a moment—wondering whether to offer to do that himself?—but I guess he's still kinda mad about the twenty thousand dollars because he just says, "Okay. We can swap over later."

I put my rifle into the resort truck, along with some sealable bags and the tooth extraction kit, and start where I left off last night. Zech offered to tow all the dead raptors outside when he was negotiating the contract, but the director fellow told him a Sanitation and Maintenance Team would be along in due course to—among other tasks—remove the carcasses from the resort's vicinity entirely—definitely the better option, avoiding a stinking heap of carrion attracting carni'saurs and horrifying the guests.

That saves us a job, but we still need to remove all the killing claws—city boys have an insatiable appetite for such 'novelties'—along with the best fangs and ruff feathers. Plus count and document them all, for the cull report.

I work quickly and pop back to the 'Vi after a couple of hours to give Zech a break. When I offer to carry on with the carcasses, he lets me, despite the fact it's been drizzling for an hour already, so, yeah, he's still pretty cheesed off.

By five o'clock, the fence is as good as new—except the innermost very definitely *un*-electrified childproof fence, but apparently that's the maintenance team's business—and as soon as the fence guys have left, Zech comes to join me. We work together without much conversation, but whereas usually it would be an easy silence, today it's kinda strained.

I should tell him the truth about what I've done, but I'm almost...scared. How's he gonna react? I mean, leaving aside brotherly scuffles and play fights, he's never spanked me or hit me, even when I was little, but I swear the twenty thousand dollars brought him to within a hair of trying to tan my hide. Somehow, I guess he managed to hang onto the fact that it's my money and my baby and bring himself to respect my decision. But this time...I'm not so sure.

What will he *do*? I mean, if he just yells, it'll be horrible, but never mind. But what if he...he's a very *practical* sort of guy, Zech. What if he just locks me in my bedroom until Stacey assumes I've changed my mind and has the abortion? I mean, if he tried to force me in there, we'd have a fight, like, for real, and that's a ghastly enough thought. But Zech's not stupid, as many a client could attest, so I doubt he'd use force. He'd pretend to accept it, let me go to bed as usual and then shut me in somehow. Or something like that. And what could I do about it? Try to shoot the lock off and kill myself with a ricochet? Yeah, 'cause that would help.

So...how would I know for sure if he'd really accepted it? Or was just biding his time?

My belly roils uncomfortably as I work. I've never gone against Zech before, I mean, not in any big decision that affects our lives. Why would I? He's taken care of me for years, the best big brother anyone could have.

But I'm not just Zech's little brother anymore. I'm also my child's father. So, yeah, I'll tell Zech. But I'll tell him after the paperwork is signed. Then it's too late, and he has to accept my decision.

I just hope he can forgive me.

A low, penetrating roar brings me awake. An allosaur? Male? Checking the door screen, I slide quietly down into the living area and open the window shutters.

Yep. That mature male allosaur I saw yesterday is pacing along the fence.

I bend to check the console. No messages, thank God. Stacey hasn't changed her mind. Since we've got the fence security fob, we can access the fence's data feed on our console, so I check the readings. All sections are up and working, no alarms have been triggered. Good.

Putting my boots on, I slip my earpiece in, sling my rifle over my shoulder and let myself out as quietly as possible.

The allosaur stands just the other side of the fence, staring into the resort, almost ten foot tall—a good size for a male. He doesn't even look at me as I approach—I guess he's used to scores of cityfolk lining this fence whenever he wanders close, squealing and taking pictures. I can just imagine it:

"Gee whizz, Larry, it's enormous! Is it a T. rex?"

"I don't know, Sherryl, but it's sure got a lot of

teeth!"

Why's he come up to the fence at all, though? Surely Trevor had enough sense not to allow anyone to throw scraps over to him? Ah, he can probably smell the raptor carcasses getting riper in the sun. Allosaurs are fearsome ambush predators but like most carni'saurs they're also opportunistic scavengers.

The allosaur drops his head and sniffs curiously at the ground along the new section. Yes, the fence guys wandered all over the area that's now out-fence while working on it. There's human scent where there isn't usually.

"Sorry, boy, no humans out there now," I tell him. "You'll have to go catch an iggy."

He raises his head, goes on a few more paces and turns to stare at the resort again. Huh. Tasty-smelling dead things, okay, but this place is always full of tasty-smelling humans, and he knows perfectly well he can't get in. What else is bugging him? I turn to look as well, trying to see it through his eyes—and other senses.

Yeah, it's silent, motionless. No kids, escaping from their chalets into the early morning, shriek as they play. No adults rousted from their beds by over-excited offspring to come quick and see the huge carni'saur. And to his sensitive nose, the absence of a single human in any of the chalets must be blaring.

Yeah, I doubt he's really conscious of *what* is

different this morning—that would take more brains than he possesses—but he registers that *something* is.

"Yeah, boy." I turn back to him. "No humans in here, either. Just Zech and me. But you wouldn't want to eat us. Whoever you tried to save for dessert would shoot you in the head, y'know. It would just spoil everyone's day."

He looks down at me at last with his huge, amber, slitted eyes, as though unused to being spoken to so calmly, and brings his nose closer to the fence, huge nostrils flaring as he tests my scent. Wind's blowing from me to him, so I can't smell him back.

"You're a fine fellow, aren't you?" I admire the steep ridges over his eyes, the magnificent, blueish-green display crest on his head, and his smooth, healthy, leathery skin. Other than those pronounced ridges, allosaurs do look very like a smaller version of a T. rex, to be fair. "Do you have a mate yet? No, you were calling for one just now. Don't worry, a handsome boy like you shouldn't have any trouble finding a lady allosaur. Just fluff up that fine crest and show off your muscles."

Raptors mate for life, nesting in springtime, while rex—which nest at any time of the year in this mild climate—simply couple and go their separate ways, the smaller male at a run, if the female's peckish. Allosaurs have a spring nesting season, same as raptors, for which period of time—and that alone—the pairs are fairly attentive to each other, the male helping to build the nest and bringing the female food while she guards it. But the larger female drives the male away shortly before it's time for the eggs to hatch, to protect her hatchlings from his inadequate fatherly instincts.

He doesn't seem to appreciate my dating advice—or maybe my calmness. Anyway, he opens his jaws wide and lets out another roar—this one pitched to make me run, not attract a mate.

When he's finished, I take my hands away from my ears. "Yes, very scary. However, thousands of volts and the rifle over my shoulder says you're not making good that threat so, yeah, I'll just stand here and admire you some more."

He stares back at me, reverting to puzzlement.

"Isaiah, when you're done communing with that dim-witted killing machine, how about a quick swim before breakfast?" Zech's voice speaks in my ear.

"Yeah, why not." Everything else is finished and we can't leave until the maintenance team arrive—and we get paid—so I might as well try the pool out at last. Especially if it makes Zech happy.

I don't like the chemical tang to the pool water—fresh lake or stream water is nicer, in my opinion—but it's nice to swim with Zech for a change, rather than one at a time. We laugh and splash each other and get downright silly, and the air feels clearer as we walk back to the 'Vi, damp and happy, like we've patched a breach. But the untold truth curls in my belly like a hibernating snake—or a full-grown she-rex, running flat-out towards our freshly patched fence.

Zech checks our current account while I boil a couple of eggs and keep an eye on his steak, then shakes his head. He notified the client that the contract was fulfilled as soon as the fence team left yesterday, and the contract states immediate payment on completion, but you wouldn't believe how many clients try to make us wait. I mean, when someone puts their life on the line for your interests, can't you just blinking well pay up as and when agreed?

"Has he at least signed the cull report and rex management claim?" I ask.

"Not yet."

"*Great.*"

The fence fob chimes as we're almost finished eating. I glance out of the window. "Looks like the maintenance team." A van and a dumper truck.

Zech checks the console again. "We still haven't been paid, so they can cool their heels out there. We'd better move the 'Vi to give them cover, in case your handsome friend comes back and rips their grilles off."

"Did you change the gate codes?" I check, as I head towards the cab.

Zech smirks. "What d'you think?"

I grin over my shoulder. He changed them immediately, I expect. Because a contract will get us paid *eventually*, unless they actually go bankrupt on us, but since we've got the fence fob there's a much simpler—and cheaper—way of ensuring we get our money promptly. And I really, really, really want to get paid promptly today, since every moment we kick our heels here is another moment for Stacey to have a change of heart—if she has one.

"Hello, maintenance truck," says Zech on the Intercar, as I start the engine and head for the gate. "Yeah, about that...we're waiting on some, er, information from the client and it won't be possible for us to open that gate until we get it. You know how it is."

The reply contains several swearwords, with "hunters" tagged on the end, but from the resigned tone they've run into this sort of situation before.

"Ah, chill out, man, we won't let anything eat you," says Zech and hangs up the Intercar mic.

I take my rifle up to the turret to make good Zech's assurance. Zech stays below to engage in a politely worded—at least from his side—exchange of thinly veiled threats that finally results in our pay arriving in our bank account and the cull report and rex management claim, both signed, in our inbox.

"Okay," says Zech. "Let's formally hand over the fence fob to these guys and be on our way. We're done here."

I try to concentrate on polishing the raptor claw in my hand, listening to the wind howling past the 'Vi's corners. Four weeks since I signed the paperwork with Stacey—and I still haven't told Zech.

I meant to tell him as soon as it was done. But then it would have been so obvious that getting him to restock and service the 'Vi while I dealt with the lawyer wasn't about efficiency and getting back out and earning as fast as possible—which I do desperately need with those medical bills arriving regular—or even about me just wanting to go alone 'cause of being an adult now, but simply about me tricking him. And he'd feel twice as betrayed. So, I thought I'd wait a few days. And then it just got harder. And harder. And harder.

The scent of rain and lightning hangs heavy in the air, and the 'Vi rocks in the wind, stabilizers or not. We wouldn't hear anything dangerous approaching, tonight.

The claw's looking good, almost ready to sell. I cleaned up Father Ben's pair of claws first of all, drilled holes in them and threaded them on a leather cord with all the correct knots. 'Cause it's not every day a city-guy shoots a raptor, and I can't help suspecting he might've regretted turning them down. The finished necklace now sits packaged ready to be mailed next time we're in-city, though the best address I could come up with was:

Father Benedict,
Diocesan visit to Our Lady of Speedy Succor shrine,
Also at Green Acres resort breach,
c/o Diocese of Exception,
Exception State

I hope he gets it, eventually. I'd have liked to include a letter, but I didn't know what to write. *How can I tell Zech?* is the biggest question on my mind, nagging at me day and night.

"Isaiah?"

I glance over at Zech, who's on the opposite side of the table cleaning some of the last raptor teeth from our Green Acres glut. "Umm?"

"Are you okay?"

Trying to focus on the claw, I nod. "I'm fine, Zech."

"Are you sure? 'Cause you haven't been yourself the last month. Are you worrying about the baby? 'Cause if so...there *is* always adoption, y'know. You're eighteen, you live in a 'Vi—no one would think badly of you."

"*I* would, but it's not that, Zech. I'm looking forward to having the baby here with us." I'm terrified out of my mind as well, mind you...

"That's what you say now." Zech rolls his eyes and sighs heavily. "You know they cry, right? All night?"

"I don't think they cry *all* night. They just need feeding regular, like a bottle-fed hatchling." No 'saur hatchling drinks *milk*, of course, but the liquid feed powder that simulates the partially digested food the parents would bring them is a similar consistency once mixed, and—depending on the exact mouth structure of the breed—a feeding bottle is usually the easiest way to administer it. "We've raised a ton of hatchlings, Zech, right from the egg. It can't be so very different. We'll be fine. Anyway, it's *my* baby. *You* don't have to get up and feed it."

"Oh yeah? If you're going to be fit for anything, I'll have to take a turn, won't I? Same as with a hatchling."

I sigh. "Thanks, Zech. I'm sure I'm gonna really appreciate the help." Okay, now I feel twice as bad.

"So, what *is* the matter?"

Uh-oh. Here's my chance...

But my cowardly mouth says, "Nothing, Zech. I'm fine."

Ugh, I'm *pathetic*. Why can't he just snoop in my messages and find out that way...no. Then *I'll* be hurt, and he'll be *twice* as hurt because I didn't tell him myself.

"Hmm." Zech tosses the tooth into the bag of clean ones and puts them to one side. "That's those done, finally." He reaches for the copy of the Hunter's Journal he picked up when we were in-city and flicks to the back. Going straight for the HabVi listings again. Still keen to keep an eye on the market, since he thinks it's only going to take us an extra couple of years to get the money together.

My insides *writhe*. I've *got* to tell him. I can't just let him carry on thinking...

"Zech?" I sound like I'm being strangled by a snake.

He lowers the magazine and eyeballs me. "Yeah?"

"There is...something I need to tell you."

"Yeah, I figured. So, what is it?"

I can't speak.

He flings the magazine down, glowering. "Since when am I such a carni'saur you can't talk to me, Isaiah? I thought we told each other everything?"

"We do." My voice squeaks. "I-I am. Telling you."

"No, you're not. You're just...suffocating, near as I can tell. Spit it out, Isaiah."

I swallow. "Well...when I told you Stacey accepted my offer...I didn't say...which offer."

Zech's face goes still as granite. "What do you mean, *which offer*? Twenty thousand dollars, right?"

I shake my head, sweat trickling down the back of

my neck. "She said no."

"She *what?*"

"She turned it down."

"Then what the *heck* did it say on those papers you signed?" Zech's eyes fill with dread.

Hands shaking, I just turn to the console, open my messages, select the Stacey thread and scroll back through all the more recent, practical exchanges until I reach the answer. Silently, Zech stalks around the table and bends to look. His fists clench. He seems to be relearning how to breathe.

"Forty thousand?" he whispers. "Forty thousand dollars, Isaiah? You gave her *everything*?"

"I had to." My voice is even quieter than his.

"Had to? No, you didn't! *You didn't!*"

"Yes, I did. I'm sorry, Zech." My voice remains very low, but the words spill out. "It was the most difficult decision I've ever made...until it wasn't anymore. When I stopped to think about how I'd feel with my money safe and my baby dead, then it was real easy. Okay, not *easy*. But simple. It was real simple, then. What else could I do? I'm sorry I didn't tell you, but I didn't want to hurt you, Zech, I just—"

"Oh yeah? You flush our new 'Vi down the head like it means *nothing* and then sit there and say you don't want to hurt me? Like heck you don't!"

"It's my *baby*, Zech—"

"And what am I, a random stranger?"

"Of course not, but if we think money's going to make us happy, we might as well feed ourselves to the nearest raptor pack right now. Money's only money, right? We can—"

"*Only money?* No, it was *forty thousand dollars!* Seven years work..."

"Or my baby's life?" My voice comes out soft but stubborn.

"*No!*" yells Zech, his nostrils white with rage. "You just gave *forty thousand dollars*, for...for..." Zech grabs his mug, "*for a blob of cells!*" He launches the mug into the far wall, where it shatters with an ear-shattering *clang-crash*, shards spraying everywhere.

I flinch...

..."*Don't, Father, please, please don't...*" *I beg.*

He doesn't listen. Never listens. He just raises his hand again...

...I'm on the floor; I fell right out of my chair when I recoiled. I lurch to my feet, fighting free of the memories. It's not our father, it's just Zech. Angrier than I've ever seen him, but still, it's Zech.

He's standing very still, face sickly in the lights, his lips pressed together. He's sorry he threw the mug, but I'm too angry to care.

"Blob of cells?" I shout. "Yeah, *it is*. And what the heck are you? What the heck am I? We're all blobs of cells, aren't we? What else? And if *this* blob of cells—" I smack my chest—"was stuck inside Stacey, about to be murdered, *you'd* give every cent you possess to save it, wouldn't you? *Wouldn't you?*"

Zech stares at me, shaking. "Yeah, yeah I would."

"Then don't blame me for doing the same for my kid, okay?"

Zech's silent for a long time. "You're going to be a way better dad than me," he says at last. "I sure hope your kid appreciates you." He turns and walks, head down, shoulders hunched, into the cab, shutting the door behind him.

I stand, staring at his closed door. I'm shaking too, hot and cold waves washing over me, bad memories nipping around my mind, trying to take me. We've never had an argument that bad. Ever. I wish I had Dinky to cuddle to take my mind off it, but she's in her new home, now. All we've got is a cageful of wild-caught piranha'saurs—if I try to pet one of those, it'll take my mind off things, all right, along with mouthfuls of my flesh.

My thoughts churn; I don't know what to do with myself. Go up to the turret, hide in my bedroom? But I'll just be alone with the memories. Finally, I sink down in the corner and rest my forehead on my knees, arms wrapping around my head. I don't cry. I want to, but I don't. I just huddle and try to make myself very small, the way I used to when my father was looking for me. I always feel safer when I'm small.

Zech's door hisses back before long. His footsteps tread across the 'Vi floor, grating and screeching on the shards of pottery. He sits beside me and puts his arms around me.

"I'm sorry I threw that mug, Isaiah," he whispers.

And then he just says, "I'm sorry," and holds me tight.

Ping.

My heart sinks. Another medical bill? I'd hoped I could save a little money by the time the baby was born, but two and a half months since I signed the paperwork and four and half months into my baby's pre-born life, I've not had much success. I'd no idea having a baby was so expensive.

Actually, some of the bills are for "stretch mark treatments" and cosmetic things like that, but I've paid them anyway. I guess if you're a model you need that stuff and I'm really not trying to ruin her life, though she obviously likes to believe that. I'm not giving her any excuse to back out, anyway. The paperwork the lawyer drew up should stop her having an abortion, but I could sue her for every cent she possessed and it wouldn't bring my kid back.

Mentally waving goodbye to my latest earnings, I

drag my chair a few feet to the console and check. Yep, for me. Stacey. I open it. A very short message.

19 Week Ultrasound.

With...an attachment. A baby photo! Finally! My heart practically escaping my mouth, I get the image up on the screen.

"Wow!"

"What?" Zech peers over my shoulder.

"Look! It's so detailed!" There's the baby's face. My eyes run over those precious features. Eyes, nose, chin, all so clear. Has the baby got Mom's dainty little nose? Or has it just not finished growing yet?

"My, my," murmurs Zech. "Just look at those little hands and feet."

I clamp my teeth together to keep from saying, *blob of cells, huh*? Let sleeping raptors lie; we've put that behind us. "It's *perfect*." The ultrasound machine we used for our mammal-stock on the farm was never this clear.

Ping. Another message. Stacey again. I open it.

It's a boy.

3

BREECH!

"So, what's the matter with you, huh?" As summer wanes, we've caught another batch of piranha'saurs to fulfill a pet store contract, but one of them is lethargic enough that I've removed it from the shoal for its protection.

I turn its little head in my leather-gloved fingers, peering into its tiny yellow eyes.

"Just let it out of the 'Vi, little bro, or cull it if you think that's kinder. We've got enough."

"There might not be much wrong with it, Zech. Let me try and figure it out."

Zech sighs and rolls his eyes but goes on loading clips for his rifle.

The months have flown past in a fog of work. We're both unanimous in wanting to earn every cent we can before the baby's arrival in the 'Vi slows things down. My *son's* arrival. In rare free moments, I stare at the ultrasound picture and turn names over in my head, but it's hard to decide. It's not like naming some hatchling. This is a person. Too awesome a responsibility, surely?

The sickly piranha'saur, as yet totally untamed, makes a half-hearted attempt to bite my gloved thumb as I ease its eyelid back for a closer look. "Hmmm. Are you low on minerals, my nippy little friend?"

I put it down on the table and head for one of the cupboards, digging around until I find the right bottle of mineral solution. As I draw off a dose into an appropriate-sized syringe, a yelp from the piranha'saur tells me it's tottered over to try and snack on Zech, the idiot.

"Come here, you ungrateful little beast." I grab it and turn it over, injecting the solution under the loose skin in its armpit as it kicks and screeches. "There. Let's see what that does for you."

Since the stuff usually kicks in rapidly, I shut it back into its individual cage rather than leave it loose. When I open the pen later, it launches itself onto my gloved hand with much healthier savagery. "Yeah, you're better. Back with your buddies, then."

I return it to Critter Cage One and grin at Zech, who's slapping a steak into the frying pan. "See. Only a mineral deficiency."

Zech rolls his eyes. "Want a steak?"

"No, thanks. You know, you're really breaking rule four, the way you eat."

Zech snorts. "No harm in eating a good chunk of meat when you're doing a hard day's work. Next, you'll tell me you're becoming vegetarian."

"Yeah, right. I know what canines and forward-facing eyes mean on a critter, thank you very much."

With less than one month to go before "B-day," things take a worrying turn—Stacey informs me that the baby is the wrong way up and that an attempt to turn it around has failed. It's looking likely to be a breech birth. Although my son is currently in the least dangerous of the possible breech positions, the doctors recommend a caesarean delivery because it's Stacey's first and her hips aren't super-wide.

Stacey refuses. Point blank.

No one wants to employ a model with a great ugly scar across her belly, you idiot! Stop going on about it or I'll give the baby away before you get here, okay?

After reading a terrifying description of how oxygen deprivation during a bad breech birth can cause brain damage to the baby, I pay out what little money I've managed to save to engage a specialist breech birth midwife—then lie awake worrying each night until exhaustion drags me into sleep.

"Come on, Isaiah." Zech slips a new clip into his rifle as fresh early morning air wafts through the turret's open windows, tickling inside my open mouth as I yawn. "Concentrate, okay? The baby's not due for another two weeks. We can finish these contracts and head for the city at the end of this week; be there in good time, buy what you need. The baby's position is no worse, the expert's ready, so stop worrying."

"It's still not as good as if he was head down," I point out.

"Hardly any difference, with the special midwife," he says impatiently. "I read that article too. Now for goodness's sake, are we going to cull these critters or not?"

"Yeah..."

We take up our positions, but before we can open fire the console pings.

"Can't you leave it until...?" Zech protests.

Too late, I'm already checking the message.

I'm having the baby.

"Zech!" My heart rate kicks up as though I've come

face-to-face with a charging triceratops.

"Huh, yeah, I see it."

"We've got to get in-city, *now!*"

"All right, all right. These contracts will have to wait. Let's go, then."

I slide down the ladder, leaving Zech closing the windows and securing the turret, and dash into the cab. The living area's already cleared for travel after driving to the cull site, and I have the stabilizers up, rear shutters closed, mirrors deployed and engine running before Zech's even made it downstairs. He staggers and flops onto the seat as I pull away before he can sit.

"It takes hours to have a baby, you know. Chill, little bro."

"We don't know when it started, Zech! And are you forgetting that we're *five hours* away?"

We've been working our way steadily closer to Amp-city, but we thought we'd have at least another week.

"All the same, chill. She signed all those papers, right?"

"Yeah, but the lawyer warned me about the...the limits of those. She's still gotta sign something once the baby's born, to actually transfer her parental rights to me. The papers mean that if she doesn't do it, I can sue her and get some of my money back—but they can't actually force her to sign. I don't think there's anything that can force her."

"Huh. That sucks. We'd better put our foot down."

"That's what I'm doing!"

Soon we get onto a proper track, one of the minor roads that formed the old road network back when towns and villages and isolated houses still dotted the countryside. Before most people withdrew behind the huge city fences, leaving little other than farms still occupied. The surface of such minor roads is poorly maintained these days, but it still allows much faster progress than being off-road, especially since the ground is increasingly damp now fall's getting going.

An hour later, we swing off the track and head up across country, aiming for a familiar shortcut—a pass through the range of craggy hill country that lies between us and Amp-city. It's a steep ascent, strewn with boulders too big even for a HabVi to clear, but we know the route between them. Loose gravel shifts under the 'Vi's huge wheels as we climb the final slope, but we reach the top easily enough.

"Hey!" Zech slaps my arm as the pass comes into sight ahead. "Stop! There's a rex."

Cursing under my breath, I ease the 'Vi to a halt and cut the engine, peering ahead. The rex stands smack in the middle of the gap, steep slopes to each side, staring in our direction.

Zech's already focusing the binos. "She-rex, fully

grown. *Phew*, she's a big girl, twenty-two foot high if she's an inch. Kinda glaring at us, actually. Guess we can go around or we can wait."

"Go around? By the time we get back down to the road and circle the hills it'll be near enough an extra three hours, Zech!"

"Fine, so we'll wait. She'll wander on her way soon enough."

I clench my jaw in frustration, but I put the parking brake on. A mature she-rex is one of the largest land predators to ever walk the planet, with a biting power of six *tons*. We don't want her mad at us.

Not if we can help it. My eyes dart from the rex, to the clock, to the rex, to the clock. It's already been well over an hour since Stacey's message. Another three hours to Amp-City at least! How long before my son is born?

After half an hour, the she-rex hasn't moved at all, not one step. She still stands, glaring our way, showing no interest whatsoever in leaving. She can't see us well because we're not moving, but she obviously knows something's here.

I've *got* to be there when the baby's born. I picture Stacey handing my kid to some social worker, signing some papers... Right, that's enough. Mrs. Rex is standing between me and my son. I start the engine.

Zech's head jerks around towards me. "Isaiah?

What are you—?"

I put my foot on the accelerator, pushing it all the way down, gritting my teeth. Let's see if T. rex like to play chicken.

"Isaiah!" yells Zech, as we gather speed. "Have you *lost your mind?* Stop!"

"If I'm not there..." I yell back. "Heck, she'll give the baby away just to spite me, Zech!"

"We won't be there if we're dead, *either!*"

"She'll move!"

"*Yeah?* And *then* what's she gonna do?" Zech grabs hold of the roof handle, bracing himself as we bounce and lurch over the rough ground, faster and faster.

"Move, you stupid animal!" I shout at the she-rex. "We just want to come past! *Move!*"

Zech flicks on all the lights, headlights, floodlights, spotlights, horn, everything, switches the external speakers onto max and starts banging his gun on the door, sending amplified metallic clanging noises in the rex's direction. I even flick the wipers on full speed.

She recoils, spooked by this assault on her senses— yeah, she's going to run...

Then she straightens, takes a couple of steps forward, flares her reddish-brown crest, opens her jaws wide and roars a challenge.

...or not.

"*Outage!*" swears Zech. "What's her problem?"

Concentrating on the ground ahead more than on the rex, I see it first, a tell-tale mound. "Argh! Since when is there a rex nest *here*?"

"Okay, now we've *got* to stop!"

The she-rex roars again and breaks into a run, heading our way. If we try to turn around, she'll be on us. "I think that fence has already gone live, Zech. We're committed."

Zech groans and clangs his rifle even louder, holding on tight with the other hand. I keep the accelerator flat on the floor, aiming for the rex. I don't want to hurt her, just make her move.

For long seconds, we tear towards each other, the rex, powerful legs pumping; the 'Vi, engine roaring...sweat trickles down my back...heck, she's not moving, we're going to collide...

At the last moment, she concludes that this object coming at her, though looking and smelling like a human-thing, is acting more like a charging triceratops and decides to treat it accordingly, leaping to the side.

I swerve away as we pass her, trying to keep out of reach, but in the mirror I see her lunge. A screech-squeak of teeth on metal—the engine whines, the wheels spinning in the gravelly dirt, struggling to drive us forward. With her jaws closed on our rear left corner, she staggers along behind us, throwing her weight backwards and sideways as she tries to bring her strange prey to the ground. I jam the wheel to the side to compensate, desperate to break her grip before she drags us over.

"I'll get the rex gun!" Grey-faced, Zech stands, but the 'Vi's wheels find a patch of solid rock and grip properly. Our sudden lurch forwards tips him back into his seat—and breaks the rex's grasp. With an ominous metallic screeching-tearing noise, we're free and gathering speed. I swerve around the looming nest and floor it again.

The she-rex bellows her fury, tossing aside the piece of metal still clamped in her jaws and giving chase. She's accelerating faster than the heavy 'Vi, her ten-inch teeth getting closer and closer to our mangled rear. But the ground ahead, thank God, is open enough that I can keep the accelerator pressed down and slowly but surely we draw ahead.

"Go on, back to your nest," I urge her. "Give me some credit for not driving straight through it!"

The instinct to protect her eggs finally outweighing her fury, the she-rex slows to a halt, casts a couple more enraged roars after us and stomps away. As we bumpety-bounce onwards Zech switches off all the lights, the speakers, and horn—but a high-pitched beeping continues.

"I thought so, we're breached! *Well done*, Isaiah!"

"How bad is it?" It's good Momma-Rex has stopped

following, because I have to slow down now to safely negotiate the steepening angle of the hillside.

Zech disappears into the living area—I'd wait with baited breath, only I'm concentrating too hard on our descent. Soon he pops his head back into the cab. "There's a hole all the way through. Piranha'saurs could get in or a very small velociraptor if it did one of their Houdini tricks. Should be easy enough to patch, though."

I take advantage of a gentler, smoother slope to reach out and silence the deafening alarm. "Since we're city-bound, why don't we just shut the cab door and worry about it when we get there?"

Zech's silent for a moment. Normally, he'd want to stop and weld at least an outer layer over the hole immediately, but that will take at least an hour. "Oh, fine. In the circumstances. I'll get what we need."

Survival having an awful lot to do with preparation, as Mister Wilson always taught us, Zech fetches the rex gun, scatter gun (for piranha'saurs), extra ammo for those and for our rifles, food, water, and my sleeping bag, piling it all in the footwell before closing and locking the cab door and settling in his seat again. If we break down and critters do come in, we've got what we need.

"I'm getting worried about your marbles, y'know," he growls, propping his socked feet on the dashboard, though his eyes continue to check the left mirror—rearview screen—right mirror, in a steady pattern. "You don't fool with a rex-mommy, little bro, and survive."

"Actually, we kinda just did," I point out. "But I'm sorry, Zech. I didn't know what else to do. If I'd realized she was nesting, well…" Would I have been prepared to go around? I've been flat-out convinced for weeks that I need to be there when the baby's born. But what I just did was pretty unfair on Zech. I mean, it's his life—and half his 'Vi, right? "I'm sorry, anyway."

"I dunno if you are, really. I think you'd do it again." He casts his eyes towards Saint Des. "Pleeeeease, Saint Des, don't let us meet any more rex today. No spinos, neither. Yeah, on second thoughts," he shoots me a look, swinging his legs to the floor again, "why don't you let me drive?"

"I'm fine driving, Zech."

"*I'm* not. Come on, stop."

I groan, but obey. Zech gets behind the wheel, and off we go again. To be fair, Zech keeps up a good speed.

"D'you really think she'll give the baby away for adoption or something if you're not there?" he asks quietly, after a while.

"I don't know, Zech, but I don't want to risk it. I'm not sure if she hates me, but she sure doesn't like me much these days. Feels like I forced her into this, I guess."

Zech snorts. "Uh, yeah, that would be her own greed, but anyway. Chill, bro. We'll be there—won't we, Saint Des?"

"Amen," is all I can say to that.

As we drive on, I can't help thinking about the close call we just had. Am I crazy to think of raising a baby in a 'Vi? Am I actually a bad dad, just for considering it? Mebbe some people would think so.

What would *Mom* think? I mean, she was happy to raise us out-city, on a farm. Not unSPARKed, but still. City people barely seem to distinguish between hunters and farmers, when it comes to questioning our sanity for living out here. Okay, hunters and farmers know the difference, and hunting's much more dangerous, but still. Dangerous enough that Mom would expect me to give my child to strangers? I don't know about that. I mean, a majority of hunters live to retire, despite what the cityfolk like to think.

Mebbe it's not what Mom thinks that matters, however much I love her. If *I* was my son, would I rather be given away, to be raised in safety, even though my father wanted me? Or would I rather stay with my dad, despite the extra risk? Assuming my dad was like Zech, not like our actual father.

Huh. When I think about it like that, it's not even a question anymore. Of course I'd want to be with my Zech-type dad. Surely that's how my son—how any kid—would feel?

Yeah, I'm *not* being a bad dad. I'm being a *good* dad. I mean, there's no guarantee he'd be safer in the city. Couples who adopt must be lovely people, but all the same. What if this wonderful adoptive family got into trouble? The father lost his job and started drinking? The mother got sick and died? They all got in a car wreck and my son was killed?

You're born, you live, you die. Doesn't matter where, it's all gonna happen, just the same.

I *can* take care of my son, and I want to, and I will—and that's how it should be.

Hold on, little man. I'm coming.

...Mom sits with a baby in her arms. Is it my baby? Yeah, it is.

"What's his name?" I ask.

She smiles. "Joshua."

"That's a nice name." I try it out. "Joshua…"

The baby giggles and waves tiny fists at me. I reach out towards him, and...

The jolt as we draw to a halt snaps me awake. How did I fall asleep? So much for being too keyed up. *Was that my baby in the dream?* Now that I'm sort-of-awake, I'm not sure. Was it even Mom? Or was it Mother Mary? That would make the child Jesus, right? But I was sure it was my baby in the dream. And Mom.

Huh, weird.

"You okay?" Zech's eyes are on the line of vehicles crawling towards the Amp-city gates up ahead.

I yawn, trying to rub the crick out of the back of my neck, coming properly awake. "Yeah, just trying to figure out a funny dream."

I grope in the glove box for our ID cards as we near the checkpoint. When we ran away from home all those years ago, my smart brother even packed our birth certificates, so when he turned eighteen, he was able to change his last name and get his ID card as Zechariah Wilson—which our father wouldn't recognize. I did the same last December. Kids still don't have to have ID cards, so until then Mister Wilson just drove us in-city no problem.

Going in-city, they're really only checking for suspected members of the dreaded Fence Saboteurs Association. Going out, for wanted criminals. But the more fully I wake up, the more I fume with impatience, though I guess we get waved through quick enough, really.

After about twenty-five minutes of never-ending city-driving, the 'Vi-park comes into sight ahead. Amp Prison Camp, as we hunters call it. About twelve years ago—well before Zech or I were around here—the city authorities put up a ten-foot chain link fence around the place. To provide security for us, they said—like any idiot ever tries to rob a 'Vi-park. Clearly it had more to do with keeping the uncouth, crazy hunters away from all the civilized cityfolk—and it was appreciated accordingly.

For years everyone expressed their feelings by clipping the gateway regularly or—if they'd had a particular bellyful of city prejudice—even driving right through it. About four years ago, the city authorities snapped. But instead of removing the hated fence, they installed heavy duty bollards all around the inside, with two particularly enormous ones on either side of the narrow entrance.

Now it's a stalemate. Hunters keep chopping holes in it all over the place to use as pedestrian exits and defeat the point of the thing, and on and off the city repair them. But it's just a 'Vi-park and we only come here when we need to, so Zech and I don't get quite so blue in the face about it as some of the guys.

Zech's kinda flushed as we turn carefully through that only one-and-a-half-'Vi-width entrance—he's embarrassed about our rex damage. Three of the four vehicles already parked up are familiar, no surprise—the fourth, from its super-rundown appearance, is a 'Vi-park hippie, one of those old codgers who roam from state to state, doing the bare minimum of hunting required to keep a 'Vi-park permit and rarely overnighting unSPARKed.

Cal the Can—or Cal the Canny as he prefers to be known—is relaxing beside his 'Vi with a beer as we drive past. He gets out of his camp chair to do a rex dance and give us an ironic thumbs up—Zech replies with a "stuff you" sort of wave, his face even redder.

"Just tell 'em it was your idiot kid brother." As we pull into a decent-enough spot, I'm already checking nothing's crept into the living area, not that it's likely, since we've been moving.

"Oh, I will," he smirks, putting on the parking brake and lowering the stabilizers. "It'll make a good story. Get ready to be laughed at."

I'm too busy heading for the console to worry about it. "Ah, most of them will laugh like chuckle'saurs, but secretly they'll think we're a pair of real hard men. I've just raised our cred loads; you'll see."

Though I reach to wake up the screen at once, I can't help glancing at the chilling sight of the breach at the top of our rear wall. The hole is barely more than a foot square, set one foot in from the corner. "At least she didn't actually rip the corner off. You're right, this won't be hard to patch."

"She almost had us over, Isaiah." Zech speaks with deadly seriousness. "*Promise* you'll be more careful with she-rex in future?"

Remembering how the 'Vi lurched and teetered, I know he's right. "Yeah, I promise."

Hey, there's a message! I swipe it open, clumsy with haste.

False alarm. I'll let you know when it's for real.

"You have got to be kidding me!" I check the time on the message. Huh, no wonder we didn't hear the *ping*—it was sent about three hours ago, the time we were wrestling with the rex.

Zech slaps a hand against the console's rim. "Typical!"

"Well...I guess it's a good thing, really. I've gotta get some...stuff." I mean, what was I gonna to do, carry the baby away wrapped in a towel?

When I ask for a "baby supplies store" the search engine, used to my normal interests, presents me with four pages of hatchling liquid feed powder, nestling nutrition pellets, incubation equipment, and even a company wanting to buy raptor embryo hide to make into little purses that are all the rage somewhere—okay, that's kinda twisted—before finally throwing up stuff for human babies.

One of the largest such stores, it turns out, is in the trade park just across the main ring highway that keeps the 'Vi-park at a safe distance from the bulk of the city. Forty-five minutes later—after being all-but-force-fed a steak by Zech—we stand outside a huge Babies! Babies!

Babies! store, staring at the pastel-colored frontage.

The broad expanses of window are filled with... baby stuff. All in pastel shades. Huge photos surround the displays, showing cute chubby babies of all nationalities being cuddled and swung in the air by mothers and fathers with nauseating looks of adoration on their faces. I gulp.

Zech approaches warily, cups his hands over his eyes, and peeks through the window. What I can see of his face takes on the expression I last saw when, while tracking an injured raptor on foot, we found ourselves peering around a pillar of rock into a raptor nesting ground. And yeah, it was nesting season.

I hurry forward and peer in as well.

Baby stuff. *Everywhere.* Huh, baby supply store, check. More cringe-worthy marketing images, left, right, and centre, each six or nine feet high. And *women.* Pregnant women, women with babies in slings, women with buggy-things, women with their mothers, their grandmothers, smiley store assistants, all with remarkably similar soppy looks on their faces...

"Oooookay." Zech straightens; steps back, eyes wide. "Okay, I'm going to go see about patching the 'Vi."

"Zech!" I stare beseechingly at him. *Come on, bro, don't abandon me here!*

"It's your baby," he says, trying to sound tough

despite the sweat on his brow. "I don't need to go in there, you do. And *somehow* we acquired a breach, remember? It needs dealing with. I'll see you later." He walks a few steps away, then relents enough to add, "Got your earpiece?"

I fish it from my pocket. "Yep."

"Okay, then. If something in there tries to eat you, I'll come and shoot it. Have fun, little bro."

"*Zech!*"

No use. He somehow makes a casual stroll look like a full-out sprint for safety as he disappears across the parking lot. Huh. He didn't abandon me to the *raptors*.

I straighten my dark camo jacket, hoping the old bloodstains don't look like what they are. If only I'd taken a shower after all that sweating-in-terror during our little 'Vi versus rex tug-of-war earlier, not that it would help since I'm sweating all over again now. At least I shaved yesterday, but I feel *naked* walking in there without my rifle. Walking *anywhere*, but especially in there. But city authorities don't like people strolling around with loaded firearms over their shoulders. And I guess they're going to stare at me bad enough as it is.

Saint Des, what about another nesting ground? I'd much rather, seriously.

Sadly, the store fails to transform itself — it's too like a nesting ground already, clearly — so drawing in a huge breath and slipping my earpiece into my ear, I think of my son, whisper a prayer to Saint Des, square my shoulders, push open the door—and walk inside.

Thirty seconds later, a terrifying store assistant—the beaming manageress, in fact—has me as firmly under her wing as a raptor matriarch with this season's most hapless juvenile as she leads me around the store, accompanied by a pack of eager-to-help mothers. At first, they'd stared at me as though a raptor *had* walked in. But once, face burning, I managed to stutter that my baby was about to be born and I needed some things, they were all over me.

With the exception of Marnie the Manageress and one unflappable grandmother, they're jumpy—and prone to giggling—so I try not to make any sudden moves. They seem to be enjoying my novelty value, but—I hunch my shoulders—am I a dangerous pet? Or a potential meal?

We stop in front of stand after stand of goods, everyone chipping in their recommendations—I under-stand about one word in three—occasionally falling silent for the store matriarch to speak. Marnie is fiftiesh, kinda white-Latino and smelling slightly of dog. I keep refusing things that don't seem necessary, which is most of them.

"And what about a stroller?" Marnie waves invitingly towards an entire parking lot full of little wheeled buggies, her kindly—but predatory—gaze on me. Does she get—what do they call it?—performance pay? "You'll want one of those, right?"

I picture myself trundling one of these puny-wheeled things back and forth over bumpy ground, while Zech stands guard in the turret. Yeah, maybe not. I mean, where would I even keep it? "Uh, I think I'd rather get a sling or something? Carry my baby."

Marnie deflates slightly. "But when the baby's bigger..."

"Just a sling for now, please."

A bewildering variety of slings passes in front of me. Some appear to be nothing but large shawls with even larger price tags, others have more in common with exoskeletal armor, with sci-fi prices. Janice—the black mom with red braids who smells of spices—and Kayla—the white mom with the blonde hair whose cloying perfume reminds me of Stacey and makes me sneeze—both favor the shawls—"...all the polls show..." The Japanese mom with the difficult name who smells of high end cleaning products is all for the exoskeleton—"...very latest in sling technology..."—while the fearless grandmother accompanying the shy mom is adamant for the hybrids—"common sense, really..."

Resigned to offending most of them, I try to make up my own mind. The shawls look more comfortable for the baby—less artificial—but I'd be terrified of the knot slipping undone, so eventually I pick a sturdy half-and-half type that's semi-structured with proper fastenings to keep it securely in place. It costs a fortune because it's designed to be used in the car as well, which apparently most of them aren't—NOT with old-fashioned airbags and you MUST read the instructions properly, Marnie and the pack tell me—but considering my lifestyle, it seems a good investment. No airbags in the 'Vi to worry about.

I reject a dozen more things that are impractical for a HabVi, but feel a deep sense of relief after finding a real, physical "Baby Care for Beginners" book, spiral-bound so it will lie open and with wipeable pages. I just hope I have time to read it before B-day happens for real!

"Do you have covered or uncovered electrical sockets in your apartment?" asks Marnie. It's becoming obvious that although I'm clearly a hunter by trade, it hasn't crossed any of their minds that the baby's going out-city with me—and I'm thinking maybe I'd better not disabuse them if I want to leave this nesting ground alive.

I picture the 'Vi. "Uh, yeah, they're uncovered."

"Well, you'd better have a set of these socket covers. For when the baby starts crawling."

"Uh...when will that be?"

"Oh, sometime between six to ten months." As the pack titter, her eyes do a double-take on my face, as though checking I really am that ignorant. "But if you get them now, then you can't be taken by surprise."

"Um...yeah, okay." I mean, I don't want to come in this place again, do I? *Ever.*

The socket covers go into the basket. Surely all I need now is a feeding bottle and some powdered milk?

Okay, sorry, "formula." And it turns out there're all sorts of other things I can buy too. I keep on saying no, though it makes me feel bad when they're being so helpful. But I'm going to have to use the money from our current account to pay for this stuff as it is, and if I go over half, I'll have to pay Zech back after our next contract. And where am I supposed to put it all, anyway? They're starting to accept that I live in a very *small* apartment, but I don't dare tell them exactly *how* small.

My earpiece squeaks slightly, receiving a signal at long range. Zech's voice follows. "Isaiah?"

"What's up, Zech?" Prudently, I raise a hand to the earpiece so the ring of she-rapt...uh, scary ladies will understand I'm not speaking to them.

"Did you see you just had another message from Stacey? It says, 'Baby's born, come get it. Central Hospital.'"

"*What?*" I gasp. "But she said—" I snatch the hand-pad out of my inner pocket and swipe at it.

"That ain't what she's saying now, bro."

Yep, there's the message! I never heard the *ping*. "I've got to get there right now! Meet me there?"

"I've only got one seam left to weld. I'll be there as soon as I've done it."

"You *what?* Oh, never mind. See you."

I pocket the hand-pad and look around at the circle of curious faces, so many skin tones, hair styles, opinions... For a moment they spin around me, scents blending with all the store smells into a bewildering cocktail, and I take a deep breath to steady myself. "Uh...thanks for your help. I've got to pay for this and dash. My son's been born!"

Through a sea of cooing and congratulations, I move determinedly to the checkout, then I pile the bags into the baby carrier thing that apparently doubles as a car seat and make my escape, shuddering as I walk away. I feel *exactly* like I've just had an extended tour of some nesting grounds, wondering the whole time if the pack's going to have a change of heart and rip me to shreds after all. Flagging down a cab on the in-city highway by more or less running out in front of it, I jump in.

If the baby store was a raptor nesting ground, the hospital is like hopping into a rabbit warren, but eventually I'm lugging my baby carrier full of stuff into the maternity ward. A nurse directs me to Stacey's private room. The door's open. I pause just out of sight, breathing hard, my hands shaking. This is it. I'm going to meet my son.

Oh God, help me to be a good father.

I walk in. Stacey's lying in the bed, a bit fuller in the body than my dim memory of her but looking like one of those marketing images in the baby store—not a hair out of place, though she's checking her face in a little mirror. But my eyes go immediately to the crib-thing near the window.

"I'm here." My voice comes out croaky.

Stacey rolls her eyes. "Yeah, I can *see* that. What took you so long?"

"I was in the baby store..." Hang on; it would've taken me exactly the same time from the 'Vi-park. Oh, never mind. *"Is he okay?"*

Another eye roll. "The baby's fine. It's had the colostrum; the rest is in that flask. They've taken a DNA sample for the records, and they said the birth certificate can be collected from reception."

My heartbeat slows a little. She's really going to let me take him. "Er, you said it was a false alarm?

"Yeah, well, I lied. I thought better of having you hovering out there and bursting in the moment the thing appeared and seeing me looking a total mess. I never want to be that sweaty and disheveled again."

She shudders.

Once again, I wish I'd showered. "So, uh, have you, um, got the..."

"The papers?" Stacey arches one of her unnaturally thin brows at me. "Yeah." She takes a familiar-looking folder off the bedside unit. "I still need to sign them, mind you."

I try not to swallow too obviously. "And, er, you're okay, too?

A hard edge enters her gaze. "Yeah, I'm fine, like you care. Anyway, pay up, and I'll sign."

Oh yeah. The last payment, which I've ever so carefully kept aside. I pull out the hand-pad, access my bank account and type in the transfer details. I show Stacey and let her watch while I hit the *confirm* button, mentally waving goodbye to the last third of my life's savings. "There. All done."

But, leaving the folder in her lap, she picks up another sheet of paper from the unit top, a curious look in her eyes. "You never asked for a paternity test."

I shrug. "Yeah, I, uh, thought about it." Embarrassingly late, but before Zech or the lawyer had to mention it. A prickle of unease runs down my spine. *Is* it my son?

"So why didn't you ask for one? You trust me that much?" Her smirk shows how stupid that would be.

"No. I just...imagine I saw a raptor stalking my

child, and I started running and running to save my child, and then when I was nearly there I realized it wasn't my child at all, I'd made a mistake. I wouldn't stop running and let the raptor have the child, would I?"

Her almost-invisible eyebrows go right up. "You don't care if it's your child or not?"

"No, I care a lot. I just...I didn't want the test. Not then." I didn't want to be tempted to keep my money and let the child die, just because it wasn't *my* child. Felt like I'd gotten too far in to be able to live with that.

"Huh." An odd look in her eyes, she holds out the paper. "Well, relax, of course it's yours. Never crossed my mind you wouldn't demand a test, so I had it done as soon as I found I was pregnant. Here."

I take the sheet with a hand that trembles slightly. I don't understand all the scientific words, but it's got my name on it. States still share certain data freely with one another, including basic DNA records. "Thanks," I whisper. Thanks for what? For having told the truth? For the test? I'm not sure.

Stacey picks up the folder, opens it, pulls the papers out and picks up a pen. Gives me one more long, thoughtful, semi-hostile look. I hardly dare to breathe. She's got the money. Surely she'll sign?

She sighs. "*Outage*, you look like a dying puppy, Isaiah. Still, my friend keeps telling me not to let your handsome face and puppy-dog eyes make me forget you spend all day, every day, killing things for a living. She thinks if I refuse to sign this you'll show up at my place in the middle of the night and blow my head off. *I think you'll just burst into tears—but I guess you might do both.*"

She speaks in a cocky, confident tone, as though dismissing her friend's paranoia about crazy hunters, but a flicker of unease lurks in her eyes. *I would never*, I want to say, but I keep my mouth shut as she concludes, "Well, I could do without either, so..."

She signs the form and thrusts it at me. "There, you crazy boy. You're now the sole parent of this very expensive baby. I wish you joy of each other. I've got months of dieting and skin treatments to look forward to."

Yeah, paid for by almost every cent I've ever earned! But I go on keeping my mouth shut and accept the paperwork, my hand shaking even more. Yep, signed in the right place. All official. I fold it carefully and secure it in an inner pocket with the paternity test results. Okay. Time to meet my son.

I walk right over and look into the cradle at last.

Tiny.

Light brown skin. It looks so soft.

Perfect little hands, gently curling.

A dusting of dark hair covers that tiny head.

A waft of clean baby-smell reaches my nose, very different from hatchling scent yet bringing it to mind. The smell of...new life...innocence?

Terror bursts over me, swallows me, like nothing ever. This little person is now my responsibility. *Mine.* I clutch the side of the crib as my legs go wobbly, staring down at my son.

Tiny eyes open and gaze up at me. Tiny brown eyes, just like mine and Zech's. Or a little lighter. The tiny lips and hands flex slightly. A slow blink.

Can he see me? His eyes are unfocused; I'm probably too far away. I lean closer, the fear washing away in a wave of enveloping, all-consuming love. He blinks again, and I reach out and touch his soft, soft cheek with my big, clumsy finger, winning a charming gurgle. My heart melts, reforming around the baby-shaped bullet that's lodged itself there.

"Yeah, if I were you, I'd take it and clear off before that Health Visitor woman shows up again. She gets one look at your, er, *house* and that baby will be in state care before you can say *rex egg facial.*"

I can't tear my eyes away from my son, though I do mutter, "*They're* illegal."

"Chill, Isaiah, it's just a saying. Well, stand there all day, for all I care."

I blink as the rest of her words sink in. "Hang on, what Health Visitor woman?"

"Scat, crazy boy. You do *not* want her catching up with you." Stacey picks up her mirror again.

A Health Visitor? Who has the power to take my son into state care? Yeah, we are *so* out of here.

I turn back to the crib—thank God I managed to skim-read "Chapter 1: How to Pick Up and Hold Your Baby" in the back of the cab—and place the baby carrier on the ground, pulling the bags out of it. *Blanket, I need a blanket...*

I fish one from a bag and lay it ready in the baby carrier, then—*oh, Saint Des don't let me drop him!*—I reach carefully into the crib and pick up my son. *Hand under head, check.* Oh my...holding him...I didn't think I could love him more, but it's overpowering. So fragile... I would die before I let anyone or anything hurt him. No question.

I want to hold him close, but Stacey's warning scares me. *Okay, down you go, little man, let's get out of here*...I lay him gently in the baby carrier and wrap the blanket around him, then tuck the precious flask away. Gathering bags in one hand and lifting the baby carrier with the other, I straighten again.

"What are you calling him?" asks Stacey when I move towards the door, though her eyes remain fixed to her mirror.

"Uh, I'm sorry; I haven't managed to decide yet."

"Well, you need to tell them so they can print the

birth certificate."

"I do?" *Oh no!*

She rolls her eyes. "One baby's going to be looking after the other baby, clearly. Yeah, you need to tell them."

I refuse to let her rudeness get to me. "Okay, thanks for mentioning it." I head for the door, but then pause. I mean, this is her baby too. "Uh, do you want to..." *...say goodbye?*

"No." She turns her head away and looks at the wall.

"Um. Okay. Good hunting...er, modeling. Whatever. Bye."

She doesn't reply. Doesn't look at me. At us.

I step outside. Stop again. After a moment I stick my head back around the door. "Stacey."

"What?"

"Don't take this the wrong way, because seriously, you're gorgeous and everything, but...don't assume that every drunk guy wants to be with you. 'Cause maybe they don't, really. So...if you've gotta behave like that, pick someone sober, okay?"

She stares at me, her mouth hanging open slightly. Has it really never occurred to her that a guy might not want to...? Then her eyes narrow, her gaze growing murderous.

Heat rushes to my face. "Not trying to make you

feel…er…bad," I mutter. "I just…um, bye, Stacey."

I duck back outside. Now she's really mad. I've got to get out of here before she sics that Health Visitor woman on me. I almost wish I'd kept quiet. Almost. My heart in my mouth in case I bump the baby carrier into anything, I hurry to the ward's main desk. "Uh, hi, my name's Isaiah Wilson. Could I get the birth certificate for my son, please?"

The receptionist's smile wilts as she looks me up and down. So, do I look too young or too rough? Both? "Uh, yeah. Ms Sardon said you were taking full custody. If you can just show me some ID and let me know your little boy's name, I can print it off for you."

"Yeah, of course." I place the baby carrier on the floor, between my legs for safety, and fish out my ID card, glad I remembered to keep it with me now we're in-city. I put it away again as she types in my details, then squeeze my eyes closed, struggling to think. My dream earlier fills my mind. Opening my eyes, I stare into the baby carrier. Yeah, it's a good name. None of the ones I've been toying with suit him better. *Thanks, Mom.* "Uh, yeah, his name's Joshua."

"That's a nice name." It feels like I could've announced my baby was called "Carni'saur" and I'd have gotten the same instant response—I guess the lady says that to everyone.

Oh well. She soon slides the birth certificate onto

the desk in front of me. "There you go."

"Thanks." I look it over. My name is the only parent name listed. That string of letters and numbers is something to do with my son's DNA code. The date is correct. The time...four hours ago! How long did Stacey spend primping before bothering to let me know? Oh well. All's well that ends well. Carefully, I fold it and put it with the other documents.

"Ms Sardon said you'd be paying the balance?"

Uh-oh. My savings account is empty. After that hellish trip to Babies! Babies! Babies! the current account isn't in a good way, either. "Um, yeah, about that. Is it possible to...I don't know, pay by installment or something?"

The receptionist's eyes narrow, but before she can reply a familiar hand deposits a card on the desk.

"Just pay the bill, little bro."

"Zech!" It's his savings account card. "Are you sure?"

He pushes the card closer to the receptionist, who's already reaching for it, though she eyes Zech even more doubtfully than she eyed me. "Just pay the bill. Call it a birthday gift."

Zech turns to peer into the baby carrier. "Look at this tiny fellow. Huh, he's kinda cute." Joshua waves his little hands and Zech crouches down properly. "Hello, teeny-weeny guy. Are you looking at your Uncle Z?"

"I called him Joshua," I tell Zech, crouching as well. "What d'you think?"

"Yeah, that's a good name. There was a Joshua in the Bible. Important guy. I think he led some people out of slavery or something. Uh, maybe. Something important, anyway."

"Oh, good."

"Mr. Wilson?" We both straighten, and the receptionist plops the card onto the desk in front of us, along with a receipt. "That's all gone through."

"Great, so, uh, it's okay to take Joshua home?" A horrible thought strikes me. "Or, uh, is there, like, *observation* or something?" *Ugh, no, we need to get out of here!*

The receptionist's lips thin and she looks us up and down again, but she says, "No, with so many people choosing home births these days, we don't worry about keeping babies in for observation anymore unless there's something wrong. He's a strong, healthy baby, and the doctor's happy for him to leave anytime."

"Thank you. We'll be on our way, then."

Zech gathers up the bags, so I pick up the precious carrier again and turn, almost walking into a trim, forty-something woman in a casual suit who's come up beside me. "Oh, sorry, s'cuse me."

I try to go around her, but she side-steps lightly in her smart trainer-pumps. "Mr. Isaiah Wilson?" She looks from me to Zech.

"Uh, yeah, that's me."

"Could I have a word? My name's Marianna Strickland. I'm the Child Health Visitor."

Panic explodes inside me, and I fight to keep it from my face. "Yeah, sure. How are you?" I hold out my hand, trying to dredge up every scrap I know about city manners and city behavior and correct pronunciation. "This is my brother, Zechariah."

She shakes my hand gingerly, though it's perfectly clean, then Zech's when, after a squint-eyed glance at me, he offers it. From the toned muscles in her hands and wrists, she's a committed gym-goer, despite her age. "Let's step over here." Ushering us across to a waiting area, she stops beside a large, sickly-looking plant.

I clutch the baby carrier's handle, my palm sweating, trying not to stare at the cat hairs stuck to her jacket sleeve.

"So," the lady begins, "the situation is, I performed a full child safety inspection at Ms Sardon's apartment two weeks ago and found everything in order. But when I popped in to check on the baby an hour or two ago, she informed me that she will not now be raising the baby, you will. *Why* she didn't tell me as soon as the two of you decided…well, anyway, these things happen. But I was hoping to catch you after finishing my other visits here."

I scratch my head and try to look puzzled. "She didn't update you? I'm sorry about that. I've only just heard about you, to be honest."

Actually, I am slightly puzzled. She *didn't* tell her? And not about the HabVi, either. I guess she knew I wouldn't pay up if the baby was taken away before I could claim him. Or maybe even cold-hearted Stacey prefers the idea of her child being raised by its father than by strangers. No…remembering that unease in her eyes…I guess she really was worried I'd show up at her door with a rifle — or ship her a live velociraptor. So she held her tongue, then tipped me off so I wouldn't blame her if Ms Strickland did catch up with me.

The enraged look on Stacey's face as I left the room flashes through my mind. She's got all my money, now. Is she mad enough to stab me in the back?

"Yes, well, these things happen," the Health Visitor repeats so gently she must be picturing some emotional break-up. "Anyway, I understand from Ms Sardon that you'll be taking some time off work while the baby's small. And she thought your brother might be helping out too?" She casts a wary look at Zech. If only he'd shaved in the last…fortnight.

"Yeah, Zech will be helping," I confirm, since that actually is true.

"Good, that's, uh, good. But I do need to perform a

child safety check on your apartment as soon as possible, you understand, and ensure you have adequate childcare arrangements for when you are… er…working." Gaze lingering on my camo jacket, she eyes me as though wondering if I understand what "child safety" even means.

Cool, Isaiah. Play it cool. "Of course. I've already got the covers for the sockets and things like that."

"You have?" She relaxes a little, an expression of pleased surprise blooming on her light-skinned face.

"Yeah, but it would be great to have you come around." I smile warmly at her, in that way that seems to make women become smiley and friendly with me, whatever their age. "I'd like to know everything's okay. When would be convenient? I had no idea about this, to be honest, so I'd love a chance to tidy up before you come, and today I'd just like to get Joshua home and settled in. Maybe tomorrow… Wait a minute; I might have something on tomorrow. Umm, what's Thursday like for you, Ms Strickland?"

"Call me Marianna. Thursday's a busy day for me, actually. Tomorrow would be better."

"Well, I *might* be free tomorrow." I can feel Zech trying to read my mind beside me, but—thank God— not knowing what's going on, he's letting me do all the talking. "But I haven't got my schedule with me. Can I call you when I get home, fix it up then?"

"Of course, here's my number, Mr. Wilson..."

"...Isaiah..."

"Isaiah." She hands me a business card. "Give me a ring and we'll get it arranged."

"Great." I place the card carefully inside my jacket as though I value it. "So, are you the person I can ask about baby care and stuff?"

"Yes, that's me. Here's the child safety information." She hands me a fat little booklet. "Do you have any questions for me now?"

"Not yet. I've been reading up. I expect I'll have some by the time I see you, though."

"I expect so. Well, I look forward to seeing you and..."

"...Joshua..."

"...Joshua—lovely—later in the week."

"Fantastic." I haven't put the baby carrier down, so now I'm able to wave cheerfully at her with the hand clutching the booklet and walk casually towards the lift. Zech follows. I shoot a glance over my shoulder, but Ms Strickland isn't anywhere near Stacey's room—yet.

"So?" Zech demands, as soon as the lift doors close. I'd take the stairs normally because I don't much like these things, but right now, *speed, speed, speed*... "What's going on with that woman? Why you so scared of her? Don't try and claim you're not; I can tell."

"Stacey says if she finds out about the 'Vi, she'll

take Joshua away; give him to strangers to raise."

Zech's brows snap together. "She can do that?"

I shrug. "Stacey said so."

Zech scowls. "You do hear about how interfering the city authorities can be. Ridiculous. I mean, the 'Vi's our home. Where are we supposed to raise him? Huh. You charmed her into your hand like a bird just now, but…she can't make that visit."

"You said it."

Rather than waste time finding the right bus and risk Marianna Strickland catching up to us, we find another cab. I speed-read the info that came with the baby sling, since that's obviously going to be quicker than the car seat. Right, the sling has to go on, then the seatbelt goes through *between* Joshua and my body—like so. Yes, that's all correct. The cab driver nods confirmation—seen it all before—and off we go.

It's a good job we didn't hang around, because no sooner are we inside the 'Vi and I've popped Joshua back into the baby carrier, he starts crying. The pitiful sound slices like a raptor's claw, pulling all my insides out—panic engulfs me.

"Hey, calm down." Zech claps me on the shoulder but eyes the baby carrier warily. "Just like with a hatchling, you said, right?"

Yeah…yeah…I've done all this before. Kinda.

I take a deep breath and consider the options. Milk?

Diaper? Hot? Cold? Company?

Okay, let's get started.

After I change Joshua, not *too* clumsily, though I've never had no hatchling that wore diapers, I warm the last of the colostrum and feed him. Then I hold him securely in one arm—he's so *tiny*—rocking him gently, trying to lull him back to sleep. Holding him close makes me happy, *so* happy. But I pick up the booklet in my other hand, anxious to find out the worst.

"So how bad is it?" Zech's been sliding a large black metal crate to and fro around the living area, clearly trying to find somewhere where it won't be too badly in the way.

"What the heck is that thing, anyway?" I demand, identifying it as the source of the metallic, new plastic reek now that Joshua's crying is dying down and my guts are back in their rightful place. "Where'd you get it?"

"From that sound system and electronics store near that…place." His shudder tells me which place he means. "It's a cradle for Joshua."

"A *cradle*?" I eye the sturdy metal latches. "I'm not putting him in *that*. It would be pitch-black in there."

"Not for *all the time*. And we can put a light inside, once we fix it down somewhere. But…it's fully soundproof, Isaiah."

"Soundproof?" My eyes dart to the rear left-hand corner of the living area, still missing a chunk of insulation and ceiling, though the armored outer skin is whole again. Okay, yeah, if there's a rex or spinosaur prowling outside, I'll stick Joshua in a soundproofed box fast enough, light or no light. It looks like it would make a nice strong refuge, too. "Huh, thanks, Zech. You think of everything."

"Hmm, wish that was true." He slides the crate up against the front end of the living area and shakes his head at it but leaves it there. "So what does the booklet say?"

"Um…" I flick through it, looking for things that seem relevant. "Okay, there's a chapter on travel safety." I read for a few minutes, still rocking Joshua, my heart growing heavier and heavier. "Phew, listen to this, Zech: 'Out-city travel is always dangerous and is inadvisable with young children. Consider taking the bullet train.

"If you must make a journey out-city with your child, keep to major, fully monitored highways and obey all highway information signs. Don't use old minor roads unless you have no choice and *never* go off-road."

"Never go off-road?" snorts Zech. "What d'they think a HabVi is built for?"

Joshua's fretful noises have died down as I read, so

I continue in a soothing tone that's the opposite of how I feel: "Never stop while out-city, unless a highway sign instructs you to do so. Always continue driving until you reach your destination or, if you get tired, pull into a secure SPARKed rest area. *Never stop anywhere else.*

"Never leave the vehicle."

"Puh, don't listen to that nonsense, Josh," Zech advises his little nephew, but Joshua's finally settled off to sleep.

"Yeah, crazy, huh?" I lower the booklet and stare at the familiar metal cupboard fronts opposite without really seeing them. If this is really what these people think...then Stacey's right. They'll consider 'Vi-life unsafe. Insane. They don't go around taking farmer's babies away, and they'd fail on a lot of this stuff too. All the same, I'm guessing they won't see it that way. They really will take him.

My heart clenches. *No! No, no, no!*

Somehow, I manage not to leap to my feet and wake Joshua up again. Instead, I lay him gently in his baby carrier before standing. "Come on, Zech! We've got to get out of here!"

Zech scratches his stubble, eyes Joshua—and smiles. "Yeah, I think we do. Let's move. We'll cancel those contracts later."

In moments, I'm in the cab re-reading the baby sling info. I could put him in the carrier, in its car seat conformation, but that will probably take even longer to fasten in correctly. And with everything that's happening, I don't want him out of my grasp.

Right, seatbelt *between* my body and Joshua—check. "Okay, we're both ready" I say, once Joshua is securely fastened to me. Oh my, he's so *little*! "Drive carefully, Zech," I beg.

Zech has refused to hold him so far, afraid he might "break him" as he puts it, but he's already hovered over him several times with a tender look in his eyes, making up silly rhymes like, "It's your Uncle *Zee*, can you see *me*?"

"Yeah, I will." Zech backs up as though driving over thin ice and pulls away smoothly, just as a small blue city-car turns off the highway into the 'Vi-park and—as though in response to seeing us moving—stops smack in the entrance.

I peer at it, my guts clenching into a knot. "*Outage*, that's *Ms Strickland* in there!"

If she's here, at the 'Vi-park…Stacey's told her. Hell hath no fury, huh? Or was she always planning this? Who cares. Nothing matters except… My arms cradle Joshua to me. His little head rests against the sling's back support; he's still sleeping, despite being moved from his carrier. He trusts me so much? *Oh God, don't let me fail him!*

Zech keeps driving. He flashes the lights and honks

long and hard. Ms Strickland flashes right back, waving bossy "stop" gestures through the grill-less in-city windscreen of her dinky car. She pulls forward a little more to clear the highway behind her but remains in front of the gateway. Seriously? She's going up against a HabVi in *that?* I can't fault her dedication, but she's got to shift herself!

Grabbing the Intercar mic in one hand, Zech flips the on switch. "Blue city-car," he barks, "you are blocking the park entrance. Please *move!*"

"Mr. Wilson, you need to stop this instant!" comes the reply from our Intercar speaker. No warmth in her voice now. "There is no question of me allowing you to take that poor baby *anywhere* in that…that *death trap!*"

"Yeah?" snaps Zech. "We like our death trap, thanks. Move before we accidentally run over your pathetic excuse for a vehicle."

"I am not moving one inch and I will call the police if you don't stop at once and hand over that poor child, you…you barbarians!"

Police? Dread grips my throat like a vice — I see the same fear reflected on Zech's face, swiftly hidden under the angry scrunching of his brows.

"Barbarians? Us? Well, we asked nicely, you baby-stealing raptor!" Zech slams his foot down on the accelerator and the 'Vi lumbers forward, gathering speed. "Hold onto him!" he yells.

My arms wrap more tightly around Joshua's tiny body. The sling shouldn't allow him to go anywhere, it's crash-tested, but still... *"Gently!"* I gasp, torn between fear of Ms Strickland and fear of what an impact might do.

"Yep…" drawls Zech as we close on the tiny blue car. We're heading straight for it—Ms Strickland stares up at the approaching juggernaut, face contorted in terror—at the last moment Zech twitches the wheel and slides us down the side of it, clipping the rear corner only—*thunk!*

Spinning like dandelion fluff, the car glances off our side—*smack!*—and is left behind as we slide through the gateway. Both impacts were minor. We're undamaged and Ms Strickland should be fine, though I can't say the same for her puny car.

Some of the guys are already spilling from their 'Vis and running to check on her, waving and giving us thumbs-ups as they go, enjoying the half-understood drama. Maybe they can delay her calling the cops—but she'll probably be too scared to unlock her doors to her "barbarian" would-be helpers, so they won't get a chance.

Joshua, having finished sucking in an immense lungful of air, begins to wail full-out, shockingly loud.

"He okay?" Zech shoots an anxious look our way.

"Just startled, I think." His little body barely

bumped against my arms, so it must've been the noise as much as anything. "*Go*, Zech!"

The nearest city gate—a small, one-lane affair mostly used by local traffic—is ten minutes away. How long will it take Ms Strickland to recover from the shock and act? *Oh God, help us! Saint Des, what can we do?* We're caught in this city like rats in a trap—the gates are the only way out.

Zech presses steadily on the accelerator, taking us as far over the speed limit as our engine and weight can achieve. Okay, we may pick up a cop car simply for speeding, but if we don't reach the gate fast we're done for anyway. My heart pounds, *thud-thud-thud-thud*, splitting my chest. After all this, am I going to lose him?

I bounce Joshua as much as the sling allows, trying to soothe him, humming to him. Slowly—astonishingly, considering my quivering terror—he quiets. Yawns.

By the time the gate comes into sight ahead, a million years later, he's sleeping peacefully again. It's not rush hour yet, though that doesn't affect the gates as much as the rest of the city, and there's no line to speak of. But…

A cop car sits by the inspection booth. I take a sharp breath. "Zech?" My voice squeaks. I feel helpless. What should we *do?*

Zech bites his lip. "It might not be anything to do with us. You know the cops sit on the gates sometimes.

And the only way out of here is…*out*."

He keeps driving. Trying not to clutch Joshua too hard, wanting to scream at Zech to turn around—irrational!—I watch the gate draw nearer.

A car further ahead stops; passes a handful of IDs into the inspection booth. The man in the booth scans them, passes them back, the car drives on.

The next car draws to a halt…same thing.

I swallow, trying to stay calm. Only one car and one cop. We can deal with this. "What you gonna do if they drop the barrier, Zech? Drive through it?" No way the puny single bar can withstand a HabVi.

"Yeah," he agrees. "Be ready to lower the cab shutters, okay?"

Our solid metal shutters are proof against his little cop pistol, no problem.

As the gate official hands the ID card back to the guy immediately in front, the cop gets out of the car, his sidearm clearly visible—then he reaches back inside and straightens, holding a fully-automatic assault rifle.

"*Outage*," hisses Zech.

Yeah, those rounds will go straight through our shutters like they're made of lard. This guy's no fool. My hand twitches, wanting to grab my gun and fight off the carni'saur that's threatening *everything*—but I can't. Rule two *and* rule six. He's another human being—just doing his job.

I swallow even harder, licking bone-dry lips, my stomach heaving. Yeah, this is another real simple decision.

"Don't try it, Zech." My voice sounds thin as a cobweb.

Zech shoots me a look as I press a kiss onto Joshua's sleeping forehead. "Yeah, I figured."

The car pulls off—the cop points the game changer at the 'Vi…and the barrier drops down ahead of us.

Zech eases forward slowly. He brings us to a halt again, about twenty feet from the flimsy bar, keeping his hands on the steering wheel as the cop approaches the driver's window with extreme caution, the rifle still trained on us—or on our heads, which is all he can really see yet, from down there.

Yeah, out of every vehicle he might have to stop, he can be quite sure this one's loaded with weapons, ammo, and people who use them regularly. I can't bring myself to let go of Josh—are these the last moments I'll ever get to hold him? That we'll be together at all?—but I try to make sure my hands are visible as well.

When the cop taps on the door, Zech opens it so he can see in, putting his hand straight back on the wheel. "Yes, Officer?"

The cop's eyes move over us rapidly, pausing on the rifles leaning in their travelling positions in the gap between the seats and on the baby sling on my front.

He's about thirty, white, with a short blond haircut that reveals a smear of what might be pink felt-tip pen on one ear. "Switch off the engine, please."

Reluctantly, Zech obeys.

The cop nods. "Yeah, we got a garbled report that this vehicle deliberately rammed some social worker's car back at the 'Vi-park. And something about a baby."

Zech swallows. "Uh, yeah, we clipped the woman's car. I mean, *I* clipped it. I was driving. Sorry 'bout that."

"Are you aware that it's an offense to drive away from the scene of an accident without exchanging insurance details?"

"Oh? Okay, um, guilty as charged, I guess. I'll, uh, just get out, shall I, and you can take me to the station? There's no need for my brother to stay, right? It wasn't anything to do with him."

For a moment, a wave of love for my big bro chokes me. My heart beats faster and faster and faster. Surely I'll pass out if it speeds up much more?

The cop screws up his face. "Weeell, since he's the one holding the kid, I wouldn't say that. Something about a kidnapped baby, is what I heard."

"Kidnapped?" snaps Zech. *"It's his baby!"*

"Is it?"

"Yes. That woman was trying to take him away from us. That's why we had to clip her."

"So it *was* deliberate?"

"Well…kinda…um, yes. I mean, she was blocking the exit."

The cop frowns. "I'm going to have to ask you to pull out of the line of traffic."

No, no, no! We do that, and we're not getting out of here, are we? I swallow. "Look, I've got the birth certificate in the glove box. Can I get it?"

The cop hesitates—nods.

Slowly, I bend forward, open the glove box and retrieve the precious paper from the little folder where we store all our important documents. I pass it to Zech, along with our IDs, and he displays them to the cop.

"Okay, so it's your baby. Why does the social worker want it? Are you abusing it?"

"Abusing him?" My arms hug Joshua protectively. "He was only *born* today, and I would *never*! It's just because we're hunters, nothing else; that's the *only* reason she wants to take him from us! Just because we live in a 'Vi!"

"You do seem kinda young to be looking after a baby, though." The cop's frowning again.

"I'm nineteen in December! And I'm his *dad!* Anyway, I've been raising hatchlings since I was eleven years old!" The cop looks unimpressed—until I add, "Waking up in the night to feed them and everything. Of course I can take care of my son!"

"And that sling, is it rated for car travel?" He eyes

Joshua's current location with disfavor.

"*Yes!* Look!" I pick up the instructions from the seat beside me and pass them to Zech to display. "I paid a heap extra for that!"

The cop purses his lips, glancing at the traffic building up behind us. Takes one hand from the rifle to scratch his head. Eyes us again. Eyes *me*. "You look like a couple of hard boys. Why'd you stop at the barrier? In that thing you wouldn't even have noticed hitting it. So why didn't you make a run for it? That question's for you, Mr. Teen Dad."

I swallow, cradling Joshua, marveling that my pounding heart doesn't wake him, trying to savor every moment we're together. "If you'd stayed in the car or just had an itsy-bitsy pistol…um" —I bite my tongue on confessing a crime of—what do they call it?—intent and carry on—"since you've got that thing" —I nod towards the rifle that's still pointing our way—"…okay, I love my son more than, *than life*, and having him taken away would be the worst thing that's ever happened to me, worse than anything, ever, but fact is, I'd rather he grew up with strangers than that he got shot here with me, today. Once you got that thing out of that car, there was no way we could make a run for it."

"Hmm." The cop scratches his head again, chewing his lip, watching me hunching around Joshua in helpless protectiveness. He's got felt-tip pen on his wrist, too. "So…why are you happy to risk your son with all those rex and raptors out there, but not with a cop's assault rifle, huh?"

I can't help snorting, at that. "Zech and I have lived out there with those rex and raptors for seven years and we're just fine. The guy who taught us our trade lived out there his whole working life until he retired with all his limbs, age seventy. But the odds of driving away from an angry cop with one of those…that's a totally different level of dangerous, right?"

A slight smile of agreement flickers across the cop's face. He hesitates. Takes a breath. Puts his hand back on the rifle. "Okay, well, I'm thinking…I'm thinking I need to ask you to pull out of the line. Because of what came through on the radio and all. But I think…yeah, I think it would be a good idea if I just walked around your vehicle and gave it a quick check over, first, like. Yeah, I'm going to do that. Now, be a good dad while I'm inspecting this rust-bucket, won't you?"

With—was that a tiny wink?—he snaps on the safety catch, slinging the weapon over his shoulder as he strolls towards the back of the 'Vi. I swallow—Zech and I look at each other.

"Good dad?" says Zech, turning the ignition key. "Heck, yeah!"

He rams the accelerator to the floor.

The barrier flies apart into at least twenty large

splinters as we hit it. The 'Vi hardly jolts, but the clattering, splintering sound makes Joshua start awake and begin drawing in a long, long breath…

Rubbing his back in pre-emptive comfort, I peer in the rearview screen. The cop stands in the middle of the lane, hands on his hips, looking after us. Not bringing the rifle up. Or reaching for his radio. After watching us for a while, he walks slowly towards his cop car. I guess he'll have to report our "escape" as soon as he gets in.

My hands shake like fall leaves as I grab all the documents and put them back into the glove box. Zech's still accelerating, pushing us right up to our top speed again, but I doubt we can outrun a cop car. Not that we'd need to—if he comes after us, we can go off-road virtually anywhere and show him a clean pair of rear mudflaps—which is why he won't bother and no one will order him to.

I glance at the highway signs passing overhead, every fifth of a mile, each bristling with the cameras Highway Control use to keep the traffic safe—but which the police can also access.

"We've got to get off the Highway, Zech."

"Yeah, I'm on it." Zech takes a hand off the wheel for a moment to re-open his door and slam it properly. "There's a minor road in half a mile."

I relax once we turn off, passing under massive signs warning that we are no longer on a monitored route, though Joshua's crying takes on an undulating note as we bump along the old asphalt. And off-road will be even worse.

"Let's stay on the track if possible," I suggest, stroking his head gently. "Shhhh, it's okay, little man."

Zech's eyes dart to my tearful burden. "Yeah. I doubt they'll bother chasing us. I mean, what are they going to do, put out road blocks?" He snorts. "Like that's going help. Anyway, if we keep on the minor roads, but avoid going in a dead straight line, I reckon we can make the border in about four hours."

Yeah, the only thing that could find us would be a chopper, and they'd still have the problem of actually catching us—and before we reach the Uty border. No, they're not going to waste their time and chopper fuel over a dented city-car, a broken barrier, and a baby that belongs with us anyway. Everyone knows chasing after hunters for minor offences is a massive waste of resources, even the cops. *Especially* the cops. They'll just shake their heads to each other, exchange some snooty city slights about "wild, uncivilized" hunters and fob Ms Strickland off with talk of "operational difficulties".

"So, where are we going?" I ask Zech. "I mean, long-term?"

Zech shrugs. "Dunno. Anywhere, right?" Anywhere but Homa, but he doesn't say that out loud.

I smile, still jiggling Joshua. "What about Exception

State? Father Ben said they're so keen to attract more hunters they've fitted up the 'Vi-park in Exception City real nice."

"Hmm, Exception? Climate's good. Not crazy hot, not crazy cold. I've heard the hunting's good, too. Lots of wild country. Let's go find out. We can always try somewhere else."

"Right. Exception State, here we come." Yeah, maybe we'll even cross paths with Father Ben.

Joshua quiets after a while despite the bumping, sleeping for almost three hours as Stacey and Ms Strickland and Amp-city fall further and further behind us. I keep an eye on the surrounding landscape, but also on the sky—just in case.

Eventually Joshua grows restless and begins to cry, so Zech pulls off the road, and I take him into the back for a quick change—a little less clumsy this time—and a feed. Mixing the "formula" is exactly like mixing the liquid feed substitute, and Josh sucks as eagerly as any fresh hatchling. I still don't want to spend the time trying to fit the car seat, and I prefer to keep him close, so when he's finished I pop him back in his sling, checking it carefully, and off we go again.

I've rarely been to this part of the state and it's good-looking country, but my gaze continually strays to that far more beautiful view, the little face looking up at me from inches away. No, I am never going to regret one cent of that money.

Dragging my eyes away, I once again check the mirrors and rear screen for 'saur activity and the sky for human. All safe. I cradle Josh's little body to me and whisper, "You're going to grow up free and happy and loved, little man."

Yeah... *Saint Des?...Mom?...God? Please don't let him ever be alone? Please let him always have people who love him?* I've always had Zech, and I want my son to have someone too. Me, preferably, but it's good to have a backup plan.

Josh's still sleeping peacefully when, early evening, we abandon the minor road—just in case—and cross the state boundary off-road, sending my spirits soaring. "Thanks, Saint Des!"

Zech, still behind the wheel, tips his head to our little statue, and on we go. We've another whole state or so to cross before we reach Exception, but we're out of Rado and that's what matters. We can go onto the main highway, now, and make much better time. We ain't killed anyone, so no cop in Uty State is gonna bother us.

Josh squirms slightly in his sleep, so insubstantial against me. The whole universe has shifted today. The future isn't mine anymore. It's his. And that's okay. More than okay.

"I would fight a she-rex for you with my bare hands, little guy," I murmur. Zech sniggers, but I don't care. Holding my son is like holding star fire in my hands. Some primeval, future-shaping force.

It feels good.

"Josh," I whisper into his tiny ear, "I love you."

===+===

If you have enjoyed this unSPARKed story, would you consider leaving a review at your favorite retailer?
Thank you!

DON'T MISS BOOKS 1-6!

OR THE OTHER PREQUEL NOVEL!

The short story
'Liam and the Hunters of Lee'Vi'
is usually free in the UK and US.
(ebook only)

JOSHUA

"Tell that hunter-boy to hurry up. I haven't got all day," snaps the man in the suit.

I glance out at the welcome party that stands on the obsoDeck. Ned Greyson, stocky and light-skinned, is Exception City Zoo's Head Raptor Keeper. I know him moderately well—the Wilson HabVi has supplied quite a few critters to this zoo over the years. The young Hispanic man—older than me but with that wet-behind-the-ears air most city-boys have—is an eager young underling, or intern, or some-such. The pretty lady—of Cheyenne heritage, I think—is the zoo vet. And there's the thin, pale man in a suit, looking down his nose at everyone, but especially at me in my camo-jacket and heavy boots. He hasn't even spoken to me. Keeps passing things through Ned.

Ned doesn't 'tell me' anything, he just screws up his face in apology and opens his hand in a 'let it go' gesture. He needn't worry. The guy's getting my goat but it takes more than that to blow my fuse.

"There we go." As Silky the velociraptor finally steps off my Habitat Vehicle's ramp into the zoo's holding pen, I press the button to lift the ramp and seal the rear door. He skitters away nervously, but by the time I've dropped out of the HabVi and climbed up to the obsoDeck to join the group standing looking down into the pen, he's run back up to the rear of the large grey vehicle where it's parked flush with the gateway, begging to be let back in, peeping plaintively like he's a juvenile again. "Sorry, Silky," I tell him, raising my voice. "This is your new home, now."

I ignore Suit-man and speak to Ned. "Yep, one velociraptor, male, adult, and zoo-tame."

Silky scratches at the 'Vi with one wing-arm claw, shoots a nervous look around at the strange pen, then calls pathetically.

"Ready to mate?" queries Ned, a twinkle in his eye.

I grin. "Yep. Though he ain't cutting a very manly figure this moment, is he? Too much new."

Ned grins too, but he looks pleased. Silky is young and healthy, virtually adult size—as tall as a wolf and several times longer from nose to tail tip—and into his adult plumage, his unusually soft, sleek charcoal grey feathers set off nicely by his dark blue ruff. A real beauty, and a perfect zoo animal.

But Suit-man steps up to the edge of the obsoDeck and peers down, making Silky start and bolt into the farthest corner of the pen. Suit-man frowns. "Well, this raptor doesn't seem very zoo-tame to me. It's terrified of everything."

"What d'you expect? He's never been in a place like this."

"We're paying extra for a raptor that isn't going to cower away from people and make the visitors think we're mistreating it. I've heard of you hunters' tricks. If you're trying to pass off some sub-standard creature on us, you won't get paid at all."

Ned winces and holds up a hand. "Now, Mr. Grundvick—"

But I don't care what Ned plans to say. Suit-man's suspicion is just one slur too many. He's gonna get punched if he keeps treating hunters like this—this guy could try even a hunter's self-restraint. But there are better ways to make a point.

"Not tame, huh?" I take two steps to the edge of the obsoDeck.

"Aw, heck, Joshua, don't you—"

I ignore Ned—and drop lightly down into the pen.

DARRYL

After knocking back my last swig of coffee, I slip on my denim jacket and pause on my way to the gun locker, checking my reflection in the hall mirror. Shoulder-length brown hair brushed—and loose, for once—face clean, blue eyes...glum. But this has happened, whether I like it or not, so I might as well make a good first impression.

"Harry, get down here, we're going to be late!"

The volume of Dad's latest bellow up the stairs shows that he means business. Well, *I'm* ready, at least.

I thought my younger brother had come around to the 'might as well make a good impression' viewpoint as well, but there's still no noise from upstairs. The fact is, when your dad comes back from a routine weekend market and supply trip to the city and announces that he's got honest-to-God *married* and that the woman—sorry, step-mom—will be coming to live with you, three weeks really isn't enough time to deal with it.

Harry totally lost it. Screamed Lord knows what at Dad, then ran off to the nearest barn. I managed not to do any screaming, but I had to go up and shut myself in the farmhouse's observation turret for almost an hour, and talk to myself *a lot*. You know: *Dad's been alone a long time, Darryl; if he's fallen in love that's wonderful, isn't it, Darryl; you want your father to be happy, don't you, Darryl?*

He totally sprung it on us, though. I guess he was so scared Potential Step-Mom—sorry, Carol—would come to her senses and decide that no handsome, propertied man of her own age was worth going and living unSPARKed on some farm. Carol's a city girl, all right.

When I finally managed to go back down and say something about being happy for Dad and try to show some interest in his new bride, he showed me a photo on his phone, and my heart didn't lift. Just sank even further. Manicured Carol looked like she'd never got within a mile of the city fence in her life, let alone stepped outside it. A less likely farmer's wife I had never seen.

Dad could tell what I was thinking, of course. Brain not completely scrambled by love. "I know Carol's no farmer, Darryl my girl," he told me, "but really, it doesn't matter, does it? We've run the farm by ourselves all this time. She can run her fashion design and consultancy business from the house—I'm getting a faster Net connection put in. And *we'll* run the farm, just as before. And you and Harry will inherit it, Darryl, no question. Carol has her own money."

I reach the gun locker and place my hand on the scanner. Much as I hated to hear Dad talking about *his will*, it's a relief to know the farm is safe. I could put up with a harem of step-moms if I had to, but if someone took the farm from me...

As I take my rifle from the rack I can't help smiling at the thought of Dad with a *harem* of Carols. No, not Dad. We're Catholic, you know. One spouse at a time. Carol's 'not religious,' apparently. I hope that won't matter. Dad did say he thinks she's 'open to it' so that's something.

I throw my ammunition sash on and check the pouches. Three hold full mags, but since we'll be traveling unSPARKed...I'll add the fourth pouch. I put my hand on the scanner to open the ammo box and take a handful of HiPiRs, or Hide Piercing Rounds. Penetrate any hide up to T. rex, these will. Though for T. rex, I really would prefer a bigger gun. *Much* bigger.

"HARRY!" roars Dad, then heads over to me. "Whoa, girl, wait up. Come on, put the rifle away."

"What?" I turn an incredulous look on him. "We're travelling unSPARKed, Dad."

"Carol's nervous enough about the trip as it is, let alone living out here. If we turn up looking like Rambo-family, she's going to freak out. I'll have my rifle. Leave yours here. Just this once."

"But why have one rifle when you can have three?" I demand.

"Most people don't take *any* weapons when they travel, Darryl."

"*City* people. And sometimes when they break down or crash, they get eaten."
"Come on, Darryl, just this once. It will make Carol feel so much better."

Dad's pleading tone is too much. I unsling my rifle from my shoulder and put it back in its place. "All right. But we'd better not end up Raptor Food."

"Of course we won't." He sounds downright cheerful with relief.

JOSHUA

"Hey, Silky-boy." I move out into the middle of the small space and drop into a crouch, making myself smaller and non-threatening as I pull a training treat from my pocket. One knee I keep bent, blocking access to my stomach, while I tuck my left wrist under my chin, palm inwards, shielding my neck. Zoo-tame ain't all the way tame, not by a long shot. "Hey, Silky-boy, Mr. Suit thinks you ain't tame enough for his liking. Poor Silky-boy. Come on, then..."

"Joshua, just come out of there," urges Ned, in a low voice.

I ignore him, too busy saying friendly things in velociraptor-speak, though I need hardly bother. Silky is already running eagerly towards me, drawn as much by my familiarity as by the treat. When he pauses a few feet away, his head on the same level as mine since I'm crouched down, I toss him the meaty drop and pull out another one. He advances again, more confidently. When he's almost close enough to grab for it, I toss it into his mouth. "Good boy. Not scared of humans, are you? Just scared of new."

He takes the last few steps and rubs his head against me, like a hatchling begging a parent for food. Yes, he's very nervous of the strange place, and it's making him even friendlier than usual.

Crooning reassuringly like an adult to a chick—but

keeping my knee and left wrist firmly in place—I stroke his charcoal grey back, healthy young velociraptor scent filling my nostrils. When he just carries on nudging me with his head and peeping anxiously, I slide an arm around him in a hug and ruffle his breast feathers, then glance at Mr. Suit.

"So, mister," I ask him, Silky's teeth inches from my face, "is this raptor tame enough for your liking?"

Get PLEASE DON'T FEED THE DINOSAURS from your favorite retailer today!

JOE

"Joe! Wake up!" K was shaking my shoulder, hard. "We're being pulled over!"

"What?" My eyes flew open. It wasn't dark, now. Light blazed around the front of the truck, and blue and red lights flashed from behind. "But you said…"

"I don't know why it's happening, but it is! We've got to jump and run. We mustn't be caught!"

He didn't need to tell *me* that! With a loud *rustle-rustle* that only we could possibly hear over the engines, he crammed my foil blanket back into his rucksack and fastened it, heaved it on. He never ever removed his gloves, but he yanked a balaclava down over his face. I did the same.

K craned his neck to get the best look outside that he could without actually showing himself.

"Argh!" he hissed. "I think it's just a random check, but the police car is herding us into a floodlit area. Police cars around it, one army truck with soldiers. Blasted French Resistance are always busy…" he added under his breath, in explanation, then went on firmly, "We've got to jump as soon as we've slowed enough, before we're surrounded. I can see forest; we run straight into it and keep going, okay? Ready?"

I swallowed. I was shaking, but I knew K was right. Jump and run like heck was our only chance. Oh *why* did they have to choose *our* truck?

"Now!"

ABOUT THE AUTHOR

Corinna Turner has been writing since she was fourteen and likes strong protagonists with plenty of integrity. Although she spends as much time as possible writing, she cannot keep up with the flow of ideas, for which she offers thanks—and occasional grumbles!—to the Holy Spirit. She is the author of over twenty-five books, including the Carnegie Medal Nominated I Am Margaret series, and her work has been translated into four languages. She was awarded the St. Katherine Drexel award in 2022.

She is a Lay Dominican with an MA in English from Oxford University and lives in the UK. She is a member of a number of organizations, including the Society of Authors, Catholic Teen Books, Catholic Reads, the Angelic Warfare Confraternity, and the Sodality of the Blessed Sacrament. She used to have a Giant African Land Snail, Peter, with a 6½" long shell, but now makes do with a cactus and a campervan.

Get in touch with Corinna...

Facebook: Corinna Turner

Twitter: @CorinnaTAuthor

www.ingramcontent.com/pod-product-compliance
Lightning Source LLC
Chambersburg PA
CBHW031010190726
48286CB00003BA/782